SLEEPERS OF MARS

Long before he wrote **The Chrysalids, The Day of the Triffids, The Kraken Wakes** and other recent successes, John Wyndham was fascinated by the future and in particular by the theme of human exploration of The Universe.

This is a collection of long short stories (or short long stories) taken from the earlier half of his writing life and which shows him even then to have been a stylist of great talent and the possessor of an imagination that was particularly fecund.

Also by the same author

The Secret People
Stowaway to Mars
Wanderers of Time

and available in Coronet Books

Sleepers of Mars

John Wyndham

writing as John Beynon Harris

Introduction by Walter Gillings

CORONET BOOKS
Hodder Paperbacks Ltd., London

Printed in Great Britain
for Coronet Books, Hodder Paperbacks Ltd.,
St. Paul's House, Warwick Lane, London, E.C.4,
by Richard Clay (The Chaucer Press), Ltd.,
Bungay, Suffolk.

ISBN 0 340 17326 2

Contents

THE FATE OF THE MARTIANS

Now that we have grown used to watching astronauts dancing on the Moon, the idea of a trip to Mars is something that most of us will concede as a possibility not far from realisation. The problems involved in such a voyage have, in fact, kept the space scientists intensely occupied for the past ten years at least, and a few ambitious theorists for a good deal longer.

The fiction writers have toyed with the notion of travelling to the planets for two centuries or more. But to foresee the day when both America and Russia would engage in systematic efforts to explore the surface of Mars, through ingenious rocket machines, with the final objective of setting human foot upon that planet, would appear to rely on something more than imaginative guesswork.

In the years before World War II interrupted his writings, the late John Wyndham was a keen observer of the first tentative experiments in rocket propulsion. While others scoffed at the prophecies of those who pioneered the science of astronautics, he lent a sympathetic ear to their aspirations—and found in them inspiration for his tales.

In *Stowaway to Mars*, his second full-length novel (already revived by Coronet Books), he anticipated the universal excitement which might one day be aroused by the attempt to cross interplanetary space—by three competing nations, in the year 1981. The story relates the adventures of the crew of the British vessel *Gloria Mundi*, which alone completes a triumphant return to Earth. An American contestant in the space race makes a disastrous landing on Mars. What happened to the crew of the Russian ship *Tovaritch*, with whom the British astronauts had a brief, unfriendly encounter? .

The first story in this new selection of the early work of John Wyndham, from the days when he wrote as John Beynon or John Beynon Harris (his real name), was intended to resolve this intriguing question. Though originally published as a sequel to the earlier novel, it is actually a separate story, in which Commander Karaminoff and his comrades discover the secrets of the mysterious red world and its perambulating machines.

Did Mars once harbour a dwindling race of beings who were compelled to take drastic measures in the face of the gradual dissolution of their panet—measures that might ensure a new lease of life for their kind? As you read the fabled history of this ancient globe and its doomed civilisation, you may be tempted to see in the efforts of the Martians to put off their inevitable fate some hint of the methods which man may have to adopt if he is to survive on his own overcrowded, polluted planet.

Unlike 'Sleepers of Mars,' the other stories in this volume saw publication in the U.S.A. before they were presented in *Tales of Wonder*, the first British magazine to specialise in science fiction, which I was able to initiate in 1937 and which became a war casualty in 1942. The notions they offer still seem fantastic, but are none the less plausible in the hands of a writer who was always noted for his ability to tell a convincing story rather than merely to project a novel idea.

WALTER GILLINGS
May 1972

Ilford, Essex.

SLEEPERS OF MARS

A Sequel to *Stowaway to Mars*

CHAPTER ONE

THE MARTIAN MACHINES

THE Sun, which has seen many strange things upon his planets, and has stranger yet to see, had risen a few hours into the Martian day at a point where, close to the equator, there was unfamiliar activity. His beams still slanted so that the wastes of reddish sandhills and protruding rocks, which cover the great part of the fourth planet, cast shadows and gave a rugged character to the scene. Before long, when he had risen a little farther, that aspect would have disappeared; the dreary miles of sand would shimmer unshaded, unchanging, barren as they had been for centuries.

All the planets are dying. Some, like Pluto swinging in his remote icy circuit, are dying without having lived. They have passed straight from glowing birth to frozen death, too far from the Sun ever to have nourished life. Not so the inner planets; certainly not so Mars. But there is nothing eternal about a star system. Those members of it which manage to produce life can sustain it only for a short time, while all the conditions are suitable. And the time left to life on Mars was growing short.

It would have been finished there long ago, but for the tenacity with which it always defends itself. Without the supreme effort which had laced the surface of the planet with canals to hold back the creeping deserts, life would have vanished thousands of years before, or would have remained only in lowly forms, close to the poles, waiting until it should be crushed at last between ice-cap and desert.

But the canals, desperate and stupendous effort though they were, could not change the inevitable. They could delay it for centuries, even millennia, as indeed they had; but they could do no more than delay. True, there was some vegetation still along their banks—dry, rusty-looking bushes, whose papery leaves rustled dismally when there was a rare breath of moving air to stir them; but even their years were numbered now. There was still water in the canals to feed their roots, and would be for a long time, but gradually they grew less.

The sky which had once been blue was now purple, growing deeper as the centuries sucked the air into space; and the ebb of the air was the ebb of life. Slowly and relentlessly, the deserts crept ever closer to the edges of the canals. . . .

But, after all, just what is meant by life? It is a pretty piece of vanity for us to assume that it is only something on a carbon basis needing oxygen for its existence. For there were things on the deserts, things in the cities and things moving in the papery bushes which suffered no inconvenience from the thining of the air. And in a part of the equatorial belt—a region where man might have been able to live even yet, had he enough atmosphere to keep his lungs working—was a manifestation that the process of decay was as yet by no means complete.

Two tall metal cylinders stood upright, separated by a space of a mile or so, their symmetry oddly alien in the featureless landscape. Both tapered at their tops to blunted noses, suggesting from a distance two colossal fingers pointing into the heavens. There was little difference in their main outlines, save that the one labelled in Russian characters close to its prow, *Tovaritch*, was supported upon four huge flanges which sprang from its base, while the slightly smaller, though more grandiosely named *Gloria Mundi* perched upon three.

About the great fins of both cylinders was a flurry of metal parts flashing in the sunlight. It gave at first a suggestion of ants at work, until a closer view showed that although the workers had, superficially, something of the form of insects, yet they belonged neither to the insect nor animal kingdoms. The likeness at a distance was an accident of design, for their coffin-shaped body-cases were supported upon three pairs of legs, while two flexible tentacles at one end gave the impression of antennae.

But the impression went little farther, for a closer view showed that the body was a metal box, no less than coffin-sized, and that the supporting legs and active tentacles were also of white metal. At the broader end, where it was natural to expect a head, was something which looked more like the front of a complicated film camera equipped with a lens which swivelled continually as it peered this way and that.

Nevertheless, there remained something insect-like in the way they fussed about the bases of the towering cylinders.

These two great rockets from Earth were not wanted on Mars, and their departure was being arranged for them. It was not, however, the callous Martian intention to drive them at random into space. The decision that they must leave held no animosity, and the activity about the flanges showed that care was being taken that both vessels should have the best possible chance of making the return to Earth safely.

It had been necessary not only to raise them from their prone positions to the perpendicular, a matter of sheer force, but there was now in progress the far more ticklish job of jacking them up and adjusting them so that the correct inclination was meticulously attained. And this precise alignment, so that the take-off performed at the exact second of a given minute should set them on the right course for Earth, was proving a matter of more difficulty with the four-flanged Russian rocket than with the tripod-supported English ship.

Nevertheless, the work was proceeding with more dispatch than the rockets' owners could have contrived, since the metallic workers, being themselves machines of precision, could dispense with much of the wearisome calculation which the men from Earth must have found necessary.

The men who had made this leap of over 35,000,000 miles across space had had the opportunity to do little more than scratch a bare acquaintance with the foreign planet. The English rocket, the *Gloria Mundi*, under the command of that spectacular and much-publicised rocket-plane racer, Dale Curtance (remember the song, 'Curty, the King of the Clouds'?), had arrived first. After landing at the spot where the rocket now stood, they had set out upon what was intended as a brief preliminary exploration as far as the banks of the near-by canal.

It had turned out to be their only expedition—and not so brief, at that. On their return, as they broke out of the scrawny canal-zone bushes on to the reddish sand, they had found their return barred by a horde of mechanical monstrosities with clearly hostile intentions. In the course of a half-night that they spent beleaguered on a sandhill, it had begun to appear that those hostile intentions would be successful by reason of the men's air or ammunition—or both—giving out.

It was the arrival of the Russian rocket which had raised the siege by scattering the weird machines in flight across the desert. The men from the *Gloria Mundi* had lost no time in taking the chance to regain their own ship.

Later, the Russians had a similar experience. Karaminoff, Comrade-Commander, had set out accompanied by five of his crew. The two others—Gordonov, the engineer, and Zhatkin, the navigating mathematician, a small, dreamy-eyed, oriental-looking man from Kirghiz—he had left in charge of the *Tovaritch*.

Karaminoff's first objective had been a visit to the other rocket. His brief interview there with Curtance was unsatisfactory to all concerned, and the affair ended in a mishap which reduced his party to four. Karaminoff had been in the act of exchanging a red flag with the hammer-and-sickle upon it for the Union Jack which the British had planted, in the ingenuous belief that its erection gave them jurisdiction over the entire planet, when an angry young man without even a respirator broke from the *Gloria Mundi*'s air-lock and fired a pistol wildly in his direction.

Luckily, the damage was not serious; the bullet had taken Mikletski, the biologist, in the flesh of his right arm. Comrade Vassiloff, second-in-command of the *Tovaritch*, had turned swiftly, and by a lucky shot disabled the young man before he could do further damage. The latter had fallen back into the air-lock and managed to pull the outer door shut behind him.

It was a misfortune, but little more than that. Real trouble came to the Russians later.

Comrade-Commander Karaminoff, unwilling to be burdened with a partially-disabled man, sent him back in company with the doctor, Platavinov, to have the wound dressed while he himself went on with three companions, Vassiloff, Vinski and Steinoi, to investigate the source of an agitation in the bushes more than a mile away.

What he had expected to find in those dry, crackling thickets he had no very clear idea, but it was certainly not the things which emerged to meet him.

The whole party stopped dead and stared as a string of machines clanked and clattered towards them. The cases which held the mechanisms were of many shapes—cubical, spherical, ovoid, pyramidal, rhomboidal and forms unnamed. None stood much higher than a man, and some considerably lower. They moved over the sand by means of stilts, skids, joined or unjoined legs—anything but wheels. Many of the appendages were odd, unmatched and grotesquely inappropriate to the designs of the machines which drove them.

The four amazed men hesitated, and then began to retreat. But before they had covered a quarter of the distance back to their ship another band of mechanical monstrosities had raced to cut off their retreat, and they found themselves beleaguered as the English party had been before them.

The situation was unpleasant, nor did it improve. Accurate firing at the machines' lenses could put them out of action, but the Russians had only a few dozen rounds between them, and it was not by any means every shot that told. After being repulsed twice with several casualties, the machines settled down to wait as though they had all the time in Mars at their disposal—which, indeed, they seemed to have, and which the men certainly had not.

But for the present it appeared there was little to be done about it : precious ammunition must not be wasted, and it would be futile as well as foolhardy to do anything which would bring them within range of the metal tentacles or the jointed arms of the mechanical travesties.

Vinski broke open the small reflex camera he was carrying, and with the mirror from its interior, heliographed to the *Tovaritch*. The answer blinked back by the searchlight was not encouraging.

Mikletski and Platavinov had also been cut off, but were at present holding out against a small band of the mechanical monsters; the other two were now bottled up in the rocket-ship with a group of similar uncouth machines waiting patiently round the air-lock. Vinski turned his attention to the *Gloria Mundi* and signalled her in English, only to learn that she too was in a state of siege.

The day wore on with only an occasional exchange of messages to relieve the monotony. For six hours the Russians lay in the sunlight which streamed down from the strange, purplish sky, ringed round by the fantastic metal contraptions. They played a waiting game, knowing full well that it was their opponents' strength, but unable to form any practicable plan. At the end of the sixth hour another message winked from the *Gloria Mundi*.

'How long will your aid hold out?'

Vinski glanced at the meter on his oxygen tank and made a rapid calculation.

'About eight hours,' he flashed back.

It was a grim prospect. Once the tanks were finished, it would be a matter of just a few minutes. No human lungs had the capacity to win the necessary amount of oxygen from the thin Martian air. Unless something was done they would have to choose between a gasping death some time during the night and a suicidal rush at the guarding machines.

After a pause the signal light from the *Gloria Mundi* began again :

'Are going to make grenades,' Vinski read. 'Tell your ship——' Then the message ceased, mysteriously.

A few minutes later Vinski's intent gaze was diverted from the rocket. Over the flank of a sandhill, a little to the right of it, poured a stream of the crazy machines. Moving at full speed they looked even more incredible than at rest.

As they lumbered and lurched along the truly imbecilic qualities of their designs were enhanced. But for the fact that his companions were with him, Vinski would have doubted his senses. Abruptly he became aware that the machines closer at hand had also caught this urge to move. As though at a signal their loose joints clattered, and in a moment they were sweeping down upon him.

Vinski, by reason of his position, had a couple of seconds' more warning than the others. With a shout he dropped his rifle and stood up. There was no time to think; he acted instinctively, and in the only way which could save him. He took two steps forward and leaped desperately to clear the rank of oncoming machines.

It was a feat which would have been impossible on Earth, but Mars made his strength superhuman. As if he were the human shell fired from a circus gun, he sailed over the onrushing machines and tumbled to the ground behind them. But his three companions had no time to jump. They went down before the charge of threshing metal arms and feet.

As suddenly as they had started, the machines ceased to fire. Some kind of madness seemed to have overtaken them. They became a tangle of flailing levers and rods, inextricably intertwined, flashing and swirling in the sunlight with giddy brilliance.

Not until then did Vinski realise that there was a new power abroad in the Martian desert. For the first time he had a sight of the coffin-shaped machines, and with them a strange, many-legged tank-like device emitting blue flashes. It was clear that it was in some way responsible for the frenzy and disorganisation which had overtaken the attackers, for the newcomers, though queerly unfamiliar, had at least a reassuring quality of rational and credible design.

If their object had been only to disperse the fantastic attackers, they had been completely successful; but if they had intended rescue, they had not. Of the four in his group, Vinski alone survived. Karaminoff, Vassiloff and Steinoi had lost their lives beneath the stamping feet of the machines.

He found their bodies there, battered almost beyond recognition, and sick at heart he set out to trudge his lonely way back to the *Tovaritch*.

CHAPTER TWO

ORDERS TO LEAVE

HE reached the ship unmolested, for the newcomers had cleared the desert of the rest of the machines. Some had got away, but most, under the influence of the blue flashes, had contrived their own destruction and now lay in masses of tangled, broken parts.

He came from the air-lock into the ship's living-room to find that the two left on board had already been joined by the doctor, Platavinov. Vinski made his report and learned that Mikletski, too, lay dead on the desert. A swinging arm of one of the fleeing machines had crushed his head as it passed.

Four out of the crew of eight were left. They had left Earth charged to explore and learn the condition of the planet, and if possible, to get into touch with any inhabitants there might be. In a few hours their number had been halved, and two of them had not yet set foot outside the ship.

By common consent they looked to Vinski for immediate guidance. None of the four was a leader by nature, but for the moment the Ukrainian, whose official status was that of re-corder and historian of the expedition, appeared to dominate by reason of his physical size.

Zhatkin, the sad-looking Kirghizian, was happiest when he was involved in his complex figuring; when not so engaged, he tended to regard the things about him with a detached studiousness of no practical value, as far as anyone could see.

Platavinov, the doctor, had the scientific mind. He observed, he inquired, he classified; he was interested in a great many things, but he did not initiate.

There remained Gordonov, the engineer. He had started as Gordon when he was christened on Clydeside. His engines and machinery were the joy and pride of his life. Save for that period when a burning sense of injustice and a passionate desire for equality of opportunity—and opportunity on a larger scale than he could find at home—had led him to be-come a Soviet citizen, he had shown little interest in things outside his profession.

So it came about that the three turned their inquiries upon Vinski—and Vinski had little to offer. It looked to him as if the expedition had come to a finish. It was unlikely that the four of them could contrive to raise their rocket to the per-pendicular, and that had to be accomplished before the return

journey could be begun. His present forecast was that they
would stay where they were until food or air failed them, and
the end came.

He wondered how the men in the English rocket saw the
situation, and was tempted to send over an offer of mutual
assistance in raising their rockets. The memory of the shooting
incident which had concluded the previous visit deterred him,
however, for the time being.

During the night, as they lay in their hammocks, came a bewildering sensation that the world about them was turning
topsy-turvy. It took the crew of the *Tovaritch* some little time
to realise that the machines outside were solving their greatest
problem for them, and were raising their ship to the vertical.
The darkness outside gave them no chance to see how it was
being done, but daylight revealed that both rockets had been
treated alike.

The four stood by one of the fused quartz windows. Little
over a mile away the shell-like shape of the *Gloria Mundi*
gleamed at them.

'At least they're making no distinctions; that's some consolation,' Gordonov said.

'A poor sort of consolation,' the doctor thought. 'It looks to
me like a pretty pointed hint that we're not welcome.'

'Nothing that has happened to us yet could give any other
impression,' said Vinski.

'But surely they can't mean to get rid of us before we've
made any contacts? They've not even heard what we've got to
say. Damn it, it's not every day that visitors turn up from
another planet,' Platavinov objected.

Vinski crossed the room. He took his mask and oxygen tank
from their locker, and put them on. The doctor, after a
momentary hesitation, did the same, and the two men stepped
into the air-lock together.

Now that the rocket stood erect, the entrance was raised
more than a hundred feet in the air. When the outer door was
open it was possible, by leaning well out, to see what was
happening around the base flanges in an area which was out of
range of the inclined windows.

A metallic chatter accosted them as they peered down. It
sounded thin and distorted in the rarefied air, but there was
no doubt that it was a mechanically-produced voice of some
kind. Looking for its source, Vinski became aware that one of
the glittering, coffin-shaped machines was standing apart from
the rest: its tentacles were extended, and its lens pointed

directly up at them.

The chattering voice seemed to emanate from some part of it. Vinski nudged his companion, and pointed. The two of them gazed at it in silence for some perplexed seconds.

'Well, I suppose it means something,' Platavinov said at last, 'but it doesn't seem to help much. Try it in English. It may have picked some up from our Empire-building friends over there.'

But the machine did not respond. However, it did occur to it, or to its operator, that not much progress was being made. The chatter broke off abruptly. With two great sweeps of the flexible metal arms it smoothed the surface of the sand before it, then with lightning movements of one tentacle it scribbled a row of characters.

'It's a trier, anyway,' said Vinski, as they watched the queer signs taking form. 'Though why it should assume we can understand its writing, when we can't get a line on its lingo, is more than I can say. As it is, not even being able to tell which way up the stuff is, we don't look like getting far.'

The machine's tentacle whipped back and curled itself close to its side. The lens swivelled and trained itself on them. It took no more than a few seconds to appreciate that its second attempt at communication had been no more successful than the first. Undismayed, it swept the sand level again.

This time it started by making a single circular impression in the middle; then, extending a tentacle from its other side, it stood motionless for some seconds, one long arm resting on the mark and the other pointing at the Sun. The upper tentacle suddenly re-curled itself. The other rapidly drew three concentric circles about the original mark. Again the second tentacle uncurled, and pointed directly at them while the first rested on the outermost of the circles.

'That's easy; and it certainly knows where we came from,' Vinski said, as they watched it draw a fourth circle to represent the orbit of Mars.

Near a point which it had made to represent the actual position of Mars, the silvery arms made a rapid sketch of their rocket-ship, pointed towards the centre of the diagram. It swivelled its lens up once more, to be sure of attention, before it very deliberately drew a line which began at Mars and ended on the Earth's orbit.

'Which seems to indicate that you were right,' Vinski said. 'They don't seem to want us here. And if this planet can show no better forms of animation than we've seen already I can't say I'm sorry.'

Platavinov nodded. There was little chance that the machine could be intending to convey anything else. He watched it as it repeated its action in a manner which dispelled all doubt. Then Vinski, assuming an expression of intense inquiry, lifted his arm and pointed towards the other rocket. The machine drew another sketch of a rocket beside the first, and from it another line to Earth's orbit.

Vinski nodded. 'So they're to be shoved off, too,' he observed.

The machine, assured that its point was taken, became active in another way. It picked up a metal rod, retired with it for some distance and then stopped to thrust it aslant into the ground. It pointed a tentacle first to the Sun, then drew it along the shadow which the rod cast; and at the end it repeated its rocket-sketching trick in the sand.

'So far, so bad,' observed Vinski. 'About as clear as dregs. What's it doing now—communing with itself? Or don't machines commune?'

With a switch of its legs, to be sure that they still watched, the machine moved again. It drew another line from the base of the rod at an acute angle to the former. At the end of it, it started sketching once more.

'Getting damned good at drawing rockets, isn't it?' Vinski went on. 'What's the point of all this?'

Platavinov frowned, then, sure that the machine had its lens on him, he carried his finger to the right, and then raised both arms suddenly. The machine below imitated exactly with its tentacles, then pointed emphatically once more to the second line.

'What——?' began Vinski, but Platavinov cut him short.

'I gather that the idea is for us to take off exactly when the shadow coincides with the second line. That should be in about three hours, at a guess. We'd better get back and see what Zhatkin has to say about it.'

They closed the outer door of the lock and shortly re-emerged into the living-room. Vinski reported briefly to the others on what had taken place.

'The first thing seems to be for Comrade Zhatkin to determine whether some three hours from now would be a possible time for taking off,' he added. 'Will you get on with that?'

Zhatkin nodded. His eyes lost their dreamy look as he glanced at the chronometer and went to fetch his slide-rule, charts and tables.

Platavinov demurred:

'Isn't the first thing to decide whether we are going to take

any notice of this—this order to leave?' He looked thoughtfully at Vinski and Gordonov. 'So far we have learned almost
nothing of Mars save that an intelligence of some kind certainly exists here. Are we justified in wasting the labour and
expense which our comrades put into the ship by going back
practically empty-handed?

'We were to establish relations with any inhabitants of the
planet. Are we to go back now and admit that we don't even
know whether there are any, save these absurd machines? We
know nothing of the flora, fauna or minerals; we have seen
nothing but a very small corner of a desert. Oughtn't we to
stay on and try to come to some understanding with the
machines themselves, even if we cannot make contact with
their masters? We could start by convincing them that we
come with only peaceful intentions.'

'I doubt whether that would interest them—particularly as
we have already destroyed a number of machines,' Vinski replied. 'In any case, why should they bother to negotiate with
us, and what sort of an agreement can one make with a
machine?'

'There's another point,' Gordonov put in. 'I'll tell you
straight, I'm not for taking off in a few hours' time. And it's
not for Platavinov's reason, either. It's because I've had no
chance to look over the ship and test her. How am I to know
that after all she's done she is in a fit condition to turn straight
round and spend another three months in space?'

'Is anything likely to be wrong?'

'Not that I know of, but there might be.'

Vinski glanced towards one of the windows. From where he
sat he could see the British rocket. He considered it thoughtfully for a while.

'The English,' he remarked at length, 'have a saying that pos-
session is nine points of the law. It is just the kind of sentiment one would expect to find in a capitalist country. Now,
neither we nor they can truthfully say that Mars has been
possessed—far from it; nevertheless, the first thing those men
in the *Gloria Mundi* did was to set up their flag and formally
annex the planet to the British Empire.

'Yes, in one way it is a matter for smiling, but in another it
is not. For when they get back they will announce their claim
to it at once. In a case like this, it is the first claim to be
published that will carry the weight; that is where their
proverb comes in. And if they are wise enough to give other
capitalist countries a title to parts of this planet, the rest of the

world will support their claim. If we make a later claim it will appear merely that we are trying to dispossess them.

'But if we make a public announcement first that Mars is the eighth and latest republic to be attached to the Soviet Union, the position is reversed. There will be trouble and disputes, of course, but it will be registered in the minds of the world that ours was the first claim. They will say, of course, that they landed here first, and therefore have the right but at least there will be a confusion of claims.

'You may not think this matters a great deal, but one day it will. Some time there will be a better method of space travel than these cumbersome rocket-ships, and the ownership of Mars will become a practical question. When that day comes, we do not wish to see it already labelled in the public mind as just another British colony—assuming that the British Empire is still in existence, of course.'

'Certainly not,' Platavinov agreed. 'And therefore you sug- gest——?'

'That we shall do a great deal more for Russia by arriving first on Earth to announce our claim than by staying here on the thin chance that we may be allowed to do a little explor- ing.'

'But can we arrive before they do?'

'There's no doubt of that. The *Gloria Mundi* is a smaller ship. She carries less reserve of fuel. There is also the fact that she was intended to carry five, and actually left with six on board.'

'Was that true, then, about the girl stowaway?' Zhatkin asked, looking up from his calculations.

'I believe so.'

'There wasn't any sign of her when we went there,' the doc- tor put in.

'They may have thrown her out,' Gordonov suggested.

Vinski thought not. 'But whether they did or not,' he went on, 'the harm was done. The rocket had to expend the extra power required to lift her weight, which means that they have even less fuel margin than they intended.

'Now, we have a much higher proportionate reserve, as Gordonov can tell you. Even if Karaminoff and the others were still with us, we could probably accelerate to a velocity of 0.5 of a mile per second more than they would dare. Whereas, with four less to lift ...' He left the obvious conclusion of the sentence to them.

'Dare?' inquired Platavinov.

'Yes, she must retain enough fuel to break her fall back to

Earth. If she uses even one pound too much in an effort to accelerate, she'll crash when she lands, and nothing can save her. Gordonov will back me up.'

'I will that,' the engineer agreed. 'There's not a doubt about it. But you don't want 0.5 of a mile more. Man, that's an awful lot. I'd say that 0.1 or even 0.10 will give us all the lead we'll need over that distance. Zhatkin'll be able to say exactly what it works out at.'

'All right,' Platavinov admitted. 'It seems a waste that we should have come so far and found out so little; but your point about getting in first is sound. Certainly the second arrival will find his thunder stolen.'

'And it'll do that Curtance good to come off second best for once,' Vinski added. 'There'll be quite a lot of satisfaction in that. Then, if the *Gloria Mundi* takes off, we do?'

Only Gordonov dissented. He still held that there ought to be some inspection of the rocket before they trusted her to take them through space again. Vinski shrugged his shoulders.

'I know it would ease your careful mind, but if we are to be kept bottled up, you'll have no chance of doing it however long we stay.'

'Let's hope we're lucky,' Gordonov grunted.

CHAPTER THREE

MAROONED ON MARS

INSIDE the *Tovaritch* there was a silence of expectation. The four men lay ready in sprung and padded hammocks. Gordonov lay gazing intently at a small circular mirror above his head; the starting and throttle control at the end of its flexible cable lay ready in his hands. The fear which had attended the outward journey, that the circular, fused quartz windows might not stand the strain, no longer troubled them. Accordingly, it had been thought safe to leave one of them unshuttered with its heavy cover screwed back to the wall, and the mirror had been so fixed that it gave him a view of the other rocket.

Zhatkin had emerged from his calculations with a figure which gave the take-off time as being identical (as far as it was possible to judge) with that indicated by the Martian machine. Every loose object had been stowed or fastened down, and the ship made ready for the journey. The men had fastened themselves into their hammocks reluctantly, facing the prospect of eleven or twelve weeks more of close imprisonment in the flying rocket with gloomy resignation.

The machines, which had persistently hung about the base flanges during the last few hours, had now withdrawn to a respectful distance. Evidently they knew what to expect from a rocket blast. And now, as far as the *Tovaritch* was concerned, everything depended on whether the *Gloria Mundi* was going to obey the instructions to leave. If so, the *Tovaritch* would also take off and race her back to Earth; if not, she would stay to see what happened, confident that her extra reserve of power gave her the advantage over her rival in all ways.

Gordonov's gaze never shifted for an instant from the small mirror. At any moment now she might start. There was the possibility of a few seconds', perhaps as much as a minute's discrepancy between Zhatkin's calculations and theirs. His fingers were on the starting knob, ready to twist it at the sight of the first flush of flame from the other rocket.

The rest waited anxiously, watching his right hand. The seconds crawled. Then came the moment.

Fire poured in a sudden flash between the other's flanges; it streaked upwards into the purplish Martian day. The *Gloria Mundi* had gone like a meteor.

On the instant Gordonov turned the knob. The *Tovaritch* trembled and leapt. Weight fell on each man inside like a physical blow, sudden, breathtaking, and then was gone. The sky outside the window wheeled giddily. Eight hammocks swung across as one. There was a shock which set each bobbing and swinging on its springs. Alternately the men were crushed upon them, or held to them only by their straps.

Outside, sand and sky churned round in a whirl as the rocket swung and rolled. It was all over in the few nightmare seconds before Gordonov had the presence of mind to switch off.

The explosive bucking ceased at once. For a moment or two the rocket swayed, then slowly and quite deliberately the living-room began to go round and round. Only the eight hammocks on their universal swingings remained steady as lockers and panels and walls fled round them. Then, with a final, jolting lurch, the *Tovaritch* came to rest.

Gordonov lay sweating and rocking gently in his hammock. 'It's a pity,' he said, with remarkable restraint, 'that I couldn't have a look at those firing tubes.'

'We must have shot about the desert like a Chinese cracker. What happened?' asked Vinski.

Gordonov shrugged. 'At a guess I'd say that the stern tubes on one side fired, and the bunch on the other side didn't—or only half of 'em did. Only a guess, though.'

'Well, we're lucky,' put in Zhatkin. 'At least we didn't blow up.'

'If you call it luck to be faced with spending the remainder of our lives—and not a very long remainder, at that—on Mars. I'm not sure that blowing up wouldn't have been more satisfactory and less uncomfortable in the long run.'

Vinski released himself from his hammock-straps and made his way to the unshuttered window.

'Here come those damned machines again. Hundreds of 'em,' he said.

'What's it doing?' asked Gordonov.

'Signalling,' said Vinski, at the window. 'It looks as if it wants to come in. It's holding some kind of tin box.'

'Well, let's have it in,' Zhatkin advised. 'If it can fit itself into the air-lock, that is. We can't stay here for ever. If the things mean to get us, they'll do it sooner or later; and if they don't, it's about time we got on speaking terms with them.'

The others nodded.

It was twenty-four hours since the mishap to the *Tovaritch*. The knowledge that it was now impossible for them to get away had given a very different aspect to their imprisonment. Before, it had been only a matter of disappointment in that it prevented them from learning more of Mars; but now they knew that, unless some outside power should help them, they were faced with living just as long as the food, air and water in the ship could sustain them—no longer.

Vinski agreed. Through the window he signed to the machine to go to the air-lock, and crossed the room to pull the lever which released the bolts on the outer door. Half a minute later the machine entered with a clatter of its metal feet on the side of the rocket.

The *Tovaritch*'s crew inspected it with nervous apprehension. It was the first time that they had been able to examine one of the mechanical monsters at close quarters, but they learned little new. The hard, silvery metal might have been any one of many alloys, and externally there was no clue to the nature of the machinery contained in the coffin-shaped body-case. Whatever it was, it was so efficient that at a yard's distance it was impossible to distinguish any hum or sound of transmission.

The machine, however, had come neither to exhibit itself

nor to indulge in an exchange of courtesies. Without waste of time, it advanced to the table and set down there the box it was carrying. Five sides of the cube were of metal, but that which faced the men was of pearly, smoky-grey glass. While one tentacle did something at the back of the box, the other reached towards a folding stool and placed it in front of the table. Then both tentacles curled back to rest by their owner's sides.

An exclamation from Vinski drew the attention of the rest from the machine to the box on the table. The grey screen had cleared, and on it appeared the life-sized head of a man, depicted with the utmost reality of which two dimensions are capable.

The face was old, but its age was indeterminate. The head bore sparse remnants of dark hair. The features were finely shaped and regular; only the ears were disproportionate, for though they were well modelled and lay close, they were abnormally large. But it was the eyes which dominated. At first sight one saw only the eyes—wide apart and dark, perhaps a little tired, more than a little sad, but for all that, alive and strong.

Vinski felt a light touch on his arm. The machine urged him in front of the box with outstretched feeler. He obeyed, and for some seconds he and the man on the glass screen stared into each other's eyes. He had a feeling that he was being searched through.

One by one the men stood before the box and endured the scrutiny. When all had taken their turns there was a pause. Each was subdued by the sense that he had been examined and considered by a mind more powerful than his own. Only Gordonov spoke: a line of English in a quiet, ruminative tone:

' "An eye like Mars to threaten and command." '

A voice came from the box on the table. At once the machine uncurled its tentacle and tapped Platavinov. He stepped forward with his eyes fixed on those of the man in the screen. Slowly, almost as if he was unaware of it, he sank on to the stool and set his arms on the table before him.

He sat there staring, unmoving and unblinking, into the other's eyes; so still that he appeared scarcely to breathe. The rest watched uneasily, aware that something novel was afoot, but puzzled as to what it might mean. It was Zhatkin who broke the spell.

'Platavinov!' he said sharply.

No statue could have remained more unmoved than the doctor.

'I don't like this,' Vinski said, taking a step forward.

A tentacle whisked through the air to bar his way. Slowly, and quite gently, it pressed him back. Gordonov leaned forward to get a better view of the doctor.

'He's a good subject. Went under at once. Don't do anything. It's usually dangerous to disturb a hypnotic trance.'

'But what's he being hypnotised for?' Vinski asked.

'We shall have to wait, but we shall undoubtedly see,' Gordonov said resignedly.

It was a full four hours before the doctor moved, and it was a simple action when it occurred. His eyes closed and his head drooped forward on his arms. The face of the stranger vanished, but the screen still remained luminous.

'He's asleep,' said Gordonov. 'Better give him half an hour at least before we wake him.'

At the end of that tantalising wait he stepped past the machine, which made no effort to stop him, and laid his hand on the sleeper's shoulder. Platavinov stirred, rubbed his eyes and yawned.

'What happened?' inquired Zhatkin.

The doctor turned to meet their intent common gaze.

'What's wrong? Why are you all looking at me like that?'

Gordonov interrupted to give him a drink. He took it gratefully.

'How do you feel?' the engineer asked, as the cup was set down.

'Pretty tired, but——'

A sudden chatter from the diaphragm in the front of the watching machine cut him short. Platavinov replied to it without a moment's hesitation. An astounded silence fell on the living-room.

'You—you answered it!' Vinski managed at last.

'I—why, so I did.' The doctor turned his bewildered face from the men to the machine, and back. 'What's happened?'

'That's what we want to know,' three voices told him together.

The machine touched a switch at the back of the box. Again the face of the stranger appeared on the screen. This time he spoke at once. Platavinov replied as though he were talking his mother tongue.

The conversation which followed, conducted in a language which abounded in odd diphthongs and unfamiliar linguals, seemed to the listeners to be of intolerable length, though in reality little more than forty minutes passed before the face again faded from the screen.

'Well?' said Vinski. 'Now let's have it.'

Platavinov gave them a brief résumé.

The man whose head they had seen was called Soantin. He had introduced himself as the governor of Hanno, the chief of the seven inhabited cities of Mars, which the doctor understood to mean in effect the ruler of Mars, in so far as ruling was necessary. He had made an explanation and part apology for hypnotising Platavinov without his consent, on the ground that it was desirable that a means of communication should be found as soon and as easily as possible.

He appreciated that the crew of the rocket could not stay where they were indefinitely, and he had learned from the machines that the *Tovaritch* was in no condition to leave without extensive repairs. Some of the blast-tubes were badly scored and would need replacement, and it would appear that the firing element in two or more of the mixing-chambers had burned away. There were also several minor defects; in fact, in his opinion, the ship had had a very lucky escape from complete destruction.

'Kind of him,' muttered Gordonov, 'considering that it was his idea, or the machines', not to give us the chance of looking over her.'

This Soantin, Platavinov went on, wished them no harm; but he refused, both for himself and for his people, to have any contact with them. Already, he said, there had been contact between one of his men and a member of the *Gloria Mundi*'s crew, and as a result this man had picked up Earthly bacteria against which he had little resistance. It was hoped to prevent the resultant complaint from spreading, but it was extremely doubtful whether the man himself would survive the experience.

It was thus impossible that the crew of the *Tovaritch* should be offered the hospitality of Hanno or of any of the other six living cities. He had, therefore, after consultation with the machines, decided to offer them accommodation in Ailiko. This city lay at no great distance to the north of them. It was in good condition, having been in occupation until quite recent times; it had, in fact, only been abandoned some 500 Martian years—a little under 1,000 Earth years—ago.

Orders had already been given to make the most recent of the community buildings there habitable once more, and the work of aeration, water and food supply was already going forward. This accommodation he offered them freely while their ship underwent repairs.

He could not say how long these repairs would take; not only was the full extent of the necessary work unknown yet, but it might entail some research into heat-resisting alloys, for Mars had been exploited until certain metals were almost unobtainable. This, unfortunately but unavoidably, would detain them for some time, and he appreciated that each day's delay would mean for them a longer journey home; but this, he assured them, need cause them misgiving only at the prospect of a longer and therefore more tedious voyage.

The ship would be restocked for them with both food and fuel. Their new quarters would be ready by the next day, and the removal of the *Tovaritch* to Ailiko would begin in the morning.

It was an offer without alternative, but at least it was generous. There was no reason save common humanity to prevent the Martians leaving them out there on the desert to starve. 'I thanked him on behalf of all of us, and told him that we would be ready,' Platavinov ended.

Vinski nodded. 'We're in his hands,' he agreed. 'And there's one good thing; we look like learning a lot more about the place than the English did.'

'What did he mean by "after consultation with the machines"?' Zhatkin wanted to know. 'How can one "consult" with a machine?'

'I don't know, but that's how he put it,' the doctor said.

'Did he mean that they share power with the machines, or that the machines are just machines and nothing more?' Zhatkin persisted.

Platavinov looked at him wearily. 'Do you think I learnt the whole state and history of the planet in a few minutes' talk? I've told you what he told me. Now, for Lenin's sake, let me get some sleep.'

CHAPTER FOUR

THE ABANDONED CITY

THE white walls of Ailiko rose sheer from the desert sand. There was no degeneration or spread of minor buildings. Like a cliff, but with a face perforated by thousands of windows, the city reared unashamed, a frank product of civilisation defying the wastes about it.

The machines which had dragged the *Tovaritch* across the desert stopped half a mile short of the buildings and let her lie at the end of the great furrow she had ploughed across leagues of sand. A single machine approached one of the windows and beckoned with a tentacle.

The men inside climbed from their hammocks, thankful that the jolting journey was over. Each collected his breathing-mask and a small bundle of personal belongings; each also, in view of their earlier experiences, took care to arm himself with a rifle and a good supply of ammunition. Vinski and Plata-vinov were further encumbered, the former by cameras and cases of films, the latter by the television-box which kept him in touch with Soantin at Hanno.

Once the four were out of the air-lock the waiting machine wasted no time; it led the way, with its odd scuttering motion, towards the break between the buildings. The men followed with a clumsy, high-stepping walk, the result of the low Mar-tian gravity.

'I wish,' said Gordonov, half to himself, as he watched the machine ahead, 'I wish I knew what that thing is. It's made of metal, and therefore it should be a machine. But is it? Isn't it possible that there is a creature of some kind inside the box, working it—like one of those deep-sea diving-suits, only made for use on land?'

'It doesn't look that way to me,' said Vinski. 'I've been won-dering whether it might possibly be something quite strange to us, say part animal and part machine.'

The engineer considered. 'I don't see how that could be.'

'Nor I. But is that any good reason why it should not be?'

They walked on in silence. The entry to the city lay like a canyon between two masses of artificial stone. The road was gritty for a few yards from the entrance, but then gave way to smooth, hard concrete. The thin winds of Mars had been un-able to drift the sand far.

It soon became clear that the block of buildings on the right was their destination. They were led round a corner, and the machine signed them to enter a large doorway which faced inward to the city across an open, paved square. When the last member of the party had crossed the threshold, the machine followed. It touched a lever on the wall, and the great door closed silently behind them.

After a minute or less, a similar door at the other end of the room swung open. The machine chattered abruptly. Platavinov put his free hand to the buckles of his mask and slipped it off.

'It's all right. Plenty of air here,' he told the rest.

They emerged from the big air-lock into what, for a first astonished moment, they took to be the open. The size of the place and the buildings which surrounded it gave that impression, until one looked up to see the glass or glass-like roof three hundred feet above.

They stood for some minutes staring up at the huge buildings and at the balconies, inter-connected by stairs and lifts, which ran along the façades. The ground space was covered with dry earth, unpaved. It appeared less like the well of a single building than like a section of the city roofed in. Platavinov turned to the machine with a question; he translated its answer for the rest.

'It says that when the city was in use this was a garden. All the buildings had gardens in the middle.'

'But for that,' said Vinski, 'they might have left it only yesterday. Abandoned a thousand years ago, and shows no sign of it! They must have been wonderful builders. It looks as if time meant very little here.'

'I should say that that is literally true,' the doctor agreed. 'Time without change means nothing, and there can have been little change here; there are no growing things any more, and there can be little weather as we know it. Just a light wind sometimes—very rarely. When you come to think of it, it is probably a good many thousand years since it even rained on Mars.'

'Yes, I suppose it is. I hadn't thought of that.'

Zhatkin took in the scene with his sad, dreamy eyes.

'I don't like this place. It's too full of ghosts. They used to live here. They used to throng those long balconies and lean over to watch their children playing in the garden down here. And they would know what the end must be; what lay in store for their children, if not for themselves. They must, I think, have been a very unhappy people. A thousand years is nothing; something of them is still here.'

Vinski grunted. 'Well, if that's how it takes you, it'd be better if you kept it to yourself. We've got to live here.'

Nevertheless, it was not only Zhatkin who felt that sad, discouraged past which clung about the buildings.

The machine led them to the top balcony by way of a lift, and down a long corridor. By the time it reached a large, sparsely furnished room, they had lost their sense of direction.

Vinski went at once to the window which filled most of one side. He found himself looking to a straight horizon across a monotony of barren sandhills.

To the left one could just manage an oblique view of some of the rusty-looking bushes which were, as far as he knew, Mars' only form of vegetation. Beyond them was a faint gleam of water; a part, he guessed, of the canal which must have been Ailiko's life-line in its latter days. To the right he could see a part of the furrow the *Tovaritch* had ploughed, but the ship herself was out of sight.

He turned back and surveyed the room, while the machine's metallic voice chattered at a closely attentive Platavinov. The furnishing was extremely simple. A few box-like stools with padded tops, a low divan against one wall and a solid cube doing duty as a table comprised most of the portable pieces. But in the walls were a great number of panels set flush, which he assumed to cover cupboards, and also a number of separate instrument boards of some kind.

The colour of both walls and furniture was a near-white, relieved by an occasional and skilfully placed coloured line or motif. The most noticeable feature of the room was a panel of pearl-grey glass, some six feet square, set on the inner wall.

At last the machine's chatter stopped, and it took itself off the way they had come. Platavinov turned to them.

'Well, it may be a Martian custom to keep visitors at considerably more than arm's length, but I don't think we shall be able to accuse them of inhospitality. According to the machine, there's not much we shall lack—if I can remember the right levers to push.'

They had, it seemed, been given the complete freedom of Ailiko. The room they were in and those close by had been put into full working order, as far as heating and services were concerned. The whole enclosed block had been given an atmosphere of close upon fifteen pounds to the square inch, and though other parts of the city had only the attenuated natural air of the planet, they were at liberty to go where they would and see what they liked.

'As long as our oxygen-tanks last,' put in Vinski.

But Platavinov was able to assure them that there was not this limitation. In each building there were stores of space-suits which had been held partly for regular use, but more against any chance failure of the atmosphere system. They could take their pick of thousands of these ready for use, and requiring only the simple charging of the air-tanks.

Food need cause them no worry. It was chemically produced

and they had yet to find out how it tasted, but he had been told that it existed in great quantities for them to take as they wished. They could get it at any time from one of the machines stationed in the basement of the building.

'But why should they leave all this stuff here to rot?' Vinski wanted to know. 'They obviously didn't desert the place in a sudden emergency.'

'But why not leave it?' Platavinov countered. 'They had a dwindling population. They were moved from here to fill up another city where there was already more than the inhabitants needed. It would be pointless for them to take more than just their personal belongings when they left here. Presumably everybody could have as much as he wanted of everything and the rest would be useless surplus, so it was just left behind. If necessary it could be fetched, I suppose, but as the birthrate clearly continued to fall, it never was necessary.'

Vinski nodded slowly. 'Yes, I see. That would be so. In a rapidly shrinking community all values would be different, of course. It's a bit difficult at first to see it from their angle when one has always thought in terms of expansion. The viewpoint——'

'Would you mind leaving the viewpoint for a bit,' Gordonov suggested. 'Platavinov mentioned food. How do we get it?'

Platavinov crossed to a row of switches on the wall and studied the curious characters over each. He selected one, pressed it and spoke at the diaphragm above.

They waited perhaps half a minute. There was a click, and a rectangular panel in the wall fell open. In the cavity behind was a row of bowls with steam rising from them.

'That's service,' said Gordonov admiringly. 'I think I'm going to like this place.'

The meal was a success. The flavours of all the dishes were strange, but for the most part, not too strange. It was evident that the chemists responsible had kept well in mind the fact that a man who eats with zest is better fed than one who is bored by dull food. It remained to be seen if they were as good at sustaining appetite as they were at inducing it; if so, there would be little to complain at in their keep.

They followed the meal by an inspection of their rooms. Very little they could have wished for was lacking, though many of the appliances struck them as odd in design and obscure in their manner of operation until one got the trick of them; and quite a number of small devices left them baffled —much, they felt, as a man who had never seen a tin-can would be at a loss to understand the use of a simple tin-opener.

The greatest unfamiliarity lay in the bareness and austerity of the rooms. The Martian custom of building in everything which could be built in and leaving no more furniture than stools, table and divan in the open gave at first a suggestion of chilly institutionalism.

On their return to the main room, Platavinov looked thoughtfully at the grey glass panel on the inner wall.

'What is it?' Vinski asked.

'Some kind of television instrument, I gather. The machine spoke about it, but I didn't follow entirely. However, it's worth having a shot at it.'

He found a small switchboard with a complicated array of controls. At the pressing of an obvious main switch the panel began to glow, but the further manipulation of the machine proved no easy matter. It was half an hour before he managed to get a steady, undistorted picture on the screen—and that was no more than a vertical view of a stretch of desert.

He turned a knob cautiously, and the ground appeared to slide swiftly to one side. He tried another; the scene blurred and vanished in a swirl.

'How does it work?' asked Gordonov curiously.

'As far as I gathered, it is quite different from the thing we use to talk to Soantin in that it needs no transmitter. The idea is that first you decide the place to be viewed, next the view-point—your own position, as it were—then you focus two beams, kind of negative and positive carriers, on to the subject and there you are.

'The first difficulty seems to be to know which knob does what. Anyway, according to the machine, it will show you anything which is going on in this hemisphere, providing that it is out of doors; the buildings are screened against it.'

'A nice tactful thought,' said Gordonov. 'Well, you might try to get us a close-up of the *Tovaritch*. I'd like to see what's going on there.'

'What about taking a look at this place Hanno, or whatever it's called, and seeing how the Martians really live?' Zhatkin suggested.

'Seems to me that the first thing to do is to get a general idea of the layout of the country and the canals,' said Vinski.

'But even before that we've got to learn how to work the damn thing,' the doctor protested, as he applied himself to the controls again.

CHAPTER FIVE

THE FATE OF THE MARTIANS

VINSKI drifted into the room. Gordonov glanced at him, and then turned his eyes back to the visi-screen on the wall to attend to the details of the method by which the machines were busy re-lining the *Tovaritch*'s stern tubes. Vinski set down the glass-like helmet which he had been carrying under one arm, unfastened the oxygen pack from his shoulders, opened the silvery overall suit which covered him and let it slip to the floor.

Crossing to the wall, he flipped over a lever, spoke the one Martian word he had acquired into the diaphragm and waited. A bowl of liquid made its appearance in the delivery cupboard. He took it out and crossed over to sit beside the engineer on the divan.

'How are they getting on?'

'Pretty well,' Gordonov told him. 'They've been filling up with stores and doing something or other in the living-room. Once they've got the firing tubes fixed I imagine they'll be able to begin refuelling. Not more than a day or two's work now, I should think.'

'Thank Lenin for that,' said Vinski, his eyes on the visi-screen. 'The sooner we're out of this morgue the better I'll like it.'

Gordonov nodded. He, too, had found that existence in Ailiko was getting on his nerves. It was, he reckoned, the sense of futility which seemed to fill the deserted city. In the first few days they had been too busy exploring it, and discovering new devices, for it to have any appreciable effect on their spirits. The new adventure had warded off the feeling of desolation.

But as familiarity grew and the things about them ceased to be intriguing novelties, that defence was lowered. That was one of the reasons why he spent so much time at the visi-screen watching the machines at work: that was practical, constructive and hopeful work. While he could keep his attention on it he could forget the decay going on around him.

They had been in Ailiko now a mere seventeen days, but to each of them it had seemed a long slice of existence. The place continually provoked unwelcome speculations: a dead city upon a dying planet which was the home of a dwindling race.

Soantin had told Platavinov that the many millions of a few

thousand years ago were now reduced to a mere handful, working out their existences in seven cities far too big for their needs, in the face of the knowledge that a few more generations must see the end. They had no hope that conditions would change or that any natural upheaval could give them a new lease of life. They foresaw their children's end as clearly as if it had been their own.

Yet they did not commit wholesale suicide. They knew what was bound to happen—and yet they went on to meet it. That, to Gordonov—and to the rest—was one of the most deadening realisations. The people of Mars had made effort after stupendous effort to prolong their life; had irrigated the planet, had built these cities, had by these means and others pushed their survival far beyond its natural term. And yet the end would be the same as if they had made none of these efforts.

But they could not let go of life even now. There was an aspect of their state which reduced them to little more than ingenious mechanical creatures, driven on by some external power. It was, they thought, their own will that they should survive. But was it? Here they were, still struggling on in the face of the fact that they knew they could not survive.

It suggested uncomfortably that man was the driven and not the driver. And the comparison between the end of Mars and the end of Earth was inescapable. It was in that that the real pang of depression lay for the *Tovaritch*'s crew. After the first few days they had found themselves subconsciously asking: What's the use?

Indeed, what was the use? Why civilise? Why build? Why try to live by a code? Why try to cross space? Why do anything if this was to be the end of it all?

They were faced with the realisation of what must come to Earth one day, as it had already come to Mars. If that were all, the logical thing would be to end it here and now. But they did not. Even more urgently than the Martians, they were driven to working out their existences. Why? And the realisation, for the first time driven home, that they had not the slightest idea why, was knocking a lot of the conceit out of four specimens of the lords of creation.

The longer they were forced to stay on this desiccated, shrivelling planet, the more powerful became the sense of their own impotence and futility. The Martians, who knew so much more than they, had been able to do nothing but stave off extinction for a few millennia—what more could Earth hope to achieve?

And that was supposing there would still be men on Earth when she should reach this stage. Soantin thought that even that would be unlikely.

'Yours is a larger planet, with a longer life,' he had said once. 'Evolution will have more time to work.' And he went on to suggest that there would probably be several successors to man, as different from him, perhaps, as he had been from the dinosaurs. It was a theory which was scarcely kinder to the vanity of his listeners than was the prospect of their race dying with their planet.

Nothing seemed worth while any longer. The Martians had attempted a way out by constructing the machines. These, they said, would be their successors, the heirs to their knowledge. Life, of a sort, created by their intelligence, would go on on Mars long after man was gone—for the machines, Soantin assured them, were alive. They were rational beings, though simple as yet. They were built of metal, because that had been the easiest and most durable material in which to work; nevertheless, they were alive, and would develop in time.

They had been made independent of their surroundings to a greater extent than any naturally evolved organism. There was something animal, but more vegetable, in the basis of their existence. Temperature and lack of air did not affect them. As long as they had water and sunlight they could, by processes of photo-synthesis, go on.

But how much did that mean? Gordonov had asked himself. The humanity of man was lost, even though his productions should survive him—and even that was just another procrastination. When the water gave out, when the sun should grow cold, the end would come just the same. . . . Why bother about them? That summed up the feeling that the place had engendered in him : why bother? But the devil of it was that one did bother, and went on bothering.

Vinski had spoken for them all when he said the sooner they got away the better. It would not solve anything, but once they were out of the place the inevitable end would seem less near and less real.

'Where have the others gone?' Vinski asked.

'I don't know,' Gordonov told him, without moving his eyes from the screen. 'The hospital, I expect. The place seems to have an unholy fascination for Platavinov.'

'Scarcely surprising, considering he's a doctor. You spent several days in the engineering shops yourself.'

'I certainly did. And nearly went mad as a result. If these

people had been content to use only simple things like steam, oil and electricity, I might have picked up some useful hints, but this weird form of power they used for all the big jobs just leaves me guessing.'

'It must be quite easily comprehensible really,' Vinski said. 'After all, our present use of electricity would be pretty bewildering to an engineer of two centuries ago.'

'A lot of help that is. Of course, it's comprehensible if you've got somebody to explain the basic principles; but I haven't, and I can't find anywhere to begin. If I'd kept on it any longer, I'd have had a brain-storm. Since then I've kept away from the damned stuff as much as possible. Unless that hospital's a lot simpler than the workshops we shall be having to tie Platavinov down before long.'

'You needn't worry about him. The place has less effect on him than on any of us. Zhatkin go with him?'

'Sure; he gets bored in here, but he can't stand wandering round on his own. Says every corner of Ailiko's crammed full of ghosts, so he trailed along with the doctor for company.'

The two made a meal of synthetic foods. After it, Gordonov went back to his occupation of watching the repair work through the visi-screen. Vinski, too, watched for a time, but soon became tired of it. He picked up the silvery suit from the floor and pulled it on again.

'I think I'll just go along and see what they're up to,' he said. 'It's better than hanging about here.'

He took up his helmet and went out. Gordonov nodded, but did not trouble to reply.

There were two ways of getting about Ailiko. Either one passed through the building's main air-lock into the open street, or one went down to the underground passages which connected the various buildings. In the days of occupation the passages had, it was obvious, been filled with air, making it possible for the inhabitants to go about all over the city without using space-suits; now there was little to choose, for the passages had no more air than the outer surface.

Nevertheless, Vinski elected to go below ground, for it offered a more direct route to the hospital. He left the lift at its lowest level, fastened the transparent, domed helmet over his head and adjusted the air supply. Then he stepped into the lock which prevented the air from the building from leaking out into the empty passages.

It was a lonely walk under the dim roof lights. He scarcely blamed Zhatkin for his nervousness and talk of ghosts. Many a time in these passages, and in the deserted rooms, halls and galleries of Ailiko, he had himself had to fight down a sudden attack of panic. Even out in the streets, under the purple sky, one was not free from these rushes of alarm.

It came, he supposed, partly from the readiness of the city to spring to life again. With nothing dismantled, nothing destroyed and everything capable of being put into use again, it was hard to realise that it had indeed been abandoned for ever.

There was no difficulty about finding his way. He had been to look at the empty hospital before, and he carried a card upon which Platavinov had written out translations of the notices occurring in the passages. One had only to identify the lettering over the various locks and refer to the card to see which building had been reached.

But it did not prove necessary for him to go all the way to the hospital to find the others. Half a mile before he reached it he saw them coming towards him down the long corridor. The light was playing in subdued reflections upon their helmets and silver suits, and upon something which they carried between them.

He met and greeted them. It was necessary to speak loudly when wearing the helmets, for though the transmitting diaphragms set in them were sensitive, the air was thin to carry the sound.

'Beginning to get worried about you. Thought you might have had an accident,' he said. 'What the devil have you got there?'

They laid their burden on the ground. It was a long, glass-like container having both ends rounded, but one smaller than the other; a streamline shape, but for the bluntness of the narrow end.

'A Martian,' Platavinov said. 'I want to have a good look at him,' he explained.

Vinski bent over the container and peered down at it. It seemed to be filled with a slightly clouded, green liquid. Through it he could make out the form of a man, still swaying slightly from the movement. The body was entirely naked, and seen through the green fluid it seemed to him an even more unpleasant sight than the ordinary hospital cadaver in its tank. The cloudiness made it difficult to distinguish details, but he could see enough to judge that the proportions of the man differed from those of terrestrial types.

'A nice ghoulish occupation you've found for yourselves. I should have thought this place was bad enough already, without taking up body-snatching as a pastime. Where did you get it?'

'I'll show you,' Platavinov offered.

'I don't know that I'm keen. In fact, I'm not. What I need just now is cheering up, and a demonstration of how the Martians disposed of their dead isn't my idea of hilarious entertainment.'

Platavinov grinned.

'Nevertheless, I think you'll be interested in this.'

Vinski gave in, reluctant but curious. They left the container where it was, and went back to the hospital entrance. Beyond the air-lock, Platavinov pulled the switches which put the building on to the lighting mains. To Vinski's surprise, he led the way past the first obvious lift to another at the end of a corridor. Vinski's second surprise was that in it they travelled down instead of up.

A dozen feet or more lower they stopped, and emerged into a small bare room. Platavinov went to a ponderous door on the farther side and swung it open. He groped for a lever inside, and the darkness beyond was relieved by long rows of dim lights.

CHAPTER SIX

IN THE VAULT

VINSKI exclaimed aloud as he stepped over the threshold. He was facing down an aisle which seemed to extend to infinity, until the row of lights ceased to be dots and became a thin, luminous line. To his left and his right the wall stretched out of sight.

The whole of the vast floor space, save that given up to aisles and supporting pillars, was taken up with just such glassy containers as the doctor and Zhatkin had been carrying. They rested there in their thousands—perhaps their hundred thousands—lying horizontal in five-tiered racks. In the closer ones it was possible to make out the pale forms, glimmering ghastly in their green covering.

But it was not entirely, nor even mainly, the great size of the place which had caused Vinski's exclamation. His gaze had fallen upon a body which lay asprawl in the aisle on his left. Close by were two vacant spaces in one of the racks.

The body was that of a woman, still quite young. Close by

were the fragments of a container which had obviously held her. The preservation was miraculous; there had been no wasting, no distortion of any kind. Vinski would have been prepared, in other circumstances, to believe that she had died no more than a few hours before. Even yet it appeared almost that she might stir and speak.

He looked questioningly at Platavinov. The doctor shook his head.

'Yes, I'm afraid I'm responsible for that. When we opened the container I had no idea of the state of affairs here, and the poor woman died. It was most unfortunate.'

'She—what?' asked Vinski stupidly.

'She died—there on the floor.'

Vinski stared at him. Slowly he turned his eyes away and let them wander over the vast hall with its acres of glass tubes. His gaze came back to the doctor.

'Are you serious, Platavinov? Are you trying to tell me that all these are not—not dead?'

Platavinov nodded in a matter-of-fact way. 'That is so. They are not dead; but neither are they alive.

'Zhatkin and I found this place by accident; this and five more floors like it below. We thought at first that it was a burial-place, and that they had used some form of mummification. After all, many men on Earth have the vanity to believe in another life, so why not here? Here, we thought, were the Martian myriads waiting for the last trump. And as it seems to me extremely unlikely that there will be a last trump or a judgment day, I thought I'd have a look at one, just to see how like or unlike us they were.

'Well, we broke open the casing, and the poor woman died there on the floor as I told you—died of suffocation before she could come to life again. It was most unfortunate.'

'It was horrible,' Zhatkin said, with a shudder.

Vinski still stared at them incredulously. 'Are you really telling me the truth? I can't believe it.'

'I don't blame you for that. I would certainly not believe it if I had not seen it myself.'

'It was horrible,' Zhatkin repeated.

'But just what has been done to these people?' Vinski demanded.

'That's what I wanted to know. So after that we went up to the hospital library to try to find out. I can't tell you why, but it didn't take long to discover how. The stuff in the containers isn't liquid; it's a heavy gas. It has the property of arresting all organic processes in anything which is immersed in it. I can't find an exact translation for the Martian name of the state it induces, because that state is unknown to us—catalepsy, suspended animation, hibernation, none of them quite meets the case.'

'And for an indefinite length of time?'

'So it appears. There's no mention of any time limit.'

'But when was it done, and why?'

'I can't answer either of those. But I can tell you that it was done on a tremendous scale, from the records up in the hospital proper.'

'And all these,' Vinski swept an arm to take in the entire vast vault; 'all these can be revived?'

'So it would seem—barring a few inevitable accidents, I suppose.'

'And one who will never be revived,' added Zhatkin, looking down at the body at their feet.

'I can't believe it.'

'Nor can I, hardly,' Platavinov agreed, 'but I'm going to test it. However, as there is only the natural air here, we were taking that one along to our own building. We'd better be getting back to it now, hadn't we?'

Vinski followed him out bemusedly. He envied Platavinov his matter-of-fact outlook. Of the four of them, the doctor had been least affected by his surroundings. He was making a number of interesting discoveries in a deserted city, and that, for him, seemed to be the long and the short of it—almost. At any rate, this sense of desolation and haunting despair which filled the place for the rest scarcely seemed to touch him.

Vinski was irritated at his own feelings. He had been brought up to think in terms of materialism, and to explain all phenomena on that basis, keeping emotional reactions in what he considered their rightful and secondary place. It disconcerted him to find them swamping him and distorting his judgment. Yet he felt that they were doing so. He felt almost ashamed of himself as he spoke again to the doctor, but he felt that he had to speak.

'Do you think it's wise to meddle with this?'

Platavinov looked at him curiously.

'What do you mean, "wise"? How could it be unwise?'

'I don't know, but it seems to me unlikely that those people were left in their trance—or whatever it is—by accident. It must have been done on purpose; that is to say, someone has decided that they are not to wake. Do we know enough of this planet to interfere with that purpose? We don't; and, candidly, I have a feeling that the whole thing would be better left alone.'

The doctor grunted contemptuously.

'You're getting superstitious, like Zhatkin. I am a man of science. I am interested in knowing how this thing has been done, and whether it has been successfully done. I do not intend to behave like an ignorant yokel. Furthermore, these people are going to be left in their "trance," except for this one man whom I intend to examine.'

'And the woman we killed,' put in Zhatkin.

'You seem to have got her on your mind. I assure you that she died without knowing anything about it. It was an unfortunate accident, that's all.'

They came back to the main underground passage. The container still lay where they had left it. Vinski, more than half ashamed now of his illogical scruples, helped to carry it. To his earthly muscles it felt strangely light to contain a man's body.

'All ready?' asked Platavinov.

The rest nodded, but not enthusiastically. It should have been a moment when active interest swamped all other feelings, but instead it found them rather fearful for reasons which none of them could explain.

Platavinov raised his hammer and brought it down on the glass casing. The container swayed on the table; the green contents swirled, the immersed body rocked gently, but the covering did not fracture.

It was twelve hours since they had brought it to their living-room. The doctor had insisted that it remain untouched for that long to enable the temperature to rise from the below zero of the vault to that of the surrounding air.

He struck again, slightly harder, but still without effect. The third blow was successful. The container split from end to end and the two halves fell apart. The heavy green gas flowed across the table-top and began to pour over the edge with an odd deliberation, like water seen on a slow-motion film. Gordonov stepped forward and filled an empty flask with it as it dripped down.

Platavinov dropped his hammer. He sprang forward. He and Vinski seized the body between them and held it upside down. The green gas streamed out of its mouth and nostrils. They carried it over to the divan and laid it there face downwards. The doctor began to work on it as if giving artificial respiration. Under the rhythmic pressure of his hands, more of the gas was expelled to drift in a thin stream to the floor.

Without pausing in his work, he instructed Zhatkin to hand him a ready-charged syringe. Swiftly he injected its contents, and then went on with his kneading.

Half an hour passed before he relaxed his efforts. The man was now breathing deeply and regularly, but consciousness had not returned. The doctor made another injection, and wrapped the body in a warm rug; then there was nothing to do but wait. The four sat round watching the man's face for the first signs of consciousness.

'He ought to be all right,' Platavinov said. 'I gather that they have a quicker method of revival, but I didn't want to risk a strange technique, and this seems to have been quite effective.'

More than an hour passed before the man's eyes opened. All four saw the lids flicker a little before they rose. No one spoke. For some seconds the eyes remained blank and unintelligent, staring at the ceiling, then with a motion made as if in spite of great weariness, the head turned to one side and the eyes met their own.

Surprise and bewilderment crept into them. The man made an effort to move. Platavinov put out a hand gently to quieten him, and said a few words which the others did not understand. The man relaxed obediently, but his eyes were still puzzled.

After a time he revived enough to speak. Platavinov understood him; the intonation was only slightly different from that he had learned from Soantin. He translated for the benefit of the rest.

'Who are you?' the Martian asked weakly.

'Friends,' the doctor told him. 'We will explain later.'

'What year is this? How long have I slept?' the man wanted to know.

Platavinov could not tell him that. He had no idea of the basis of the Martian calendar. He replied:

'A very long time. I don't know how long.'

'Three centuries?' suggested the other. 'They said it might be for three centuries.'

The doctor could only shake his head, a gesture which seemed to puzzle the other. There was a pause, then:

'The canals? They've built the canals?' the man asked. The doctor took it as a cue.

'Oh yes. They've built the canals,' he assured him.

'That is good. Then it has been worth it,' said the Martian. Seemingly satisfied, he let his eyes close. In a few minutes he was in a natural sleep.

Platavinov looked at the others with an expression of awe and amazement.

'Before the canals were built!' he whispered. 'How many thousands of years was that, I wonder?'

CHAPTER SEVEN

THE SLEEPER'S STORY

'COME,' said Platavinov. 'It's time you had some food.'

The Martian turned obediently back from the window. He came across the room as though he were not even yet fully awake.

'This *cannot* be Ailiko,' he repeated dazedly.

'It is,' the doctor assured him patiently for the third or fourth time.

'But that desert out there; it seems to go on for ever. There was no desert at Ailiko. Where does it end?'

'I don't know. I don't think it does. I think it is all desert except for little strips beside the canals.'

'The canals; yes, the canals. But they were to be built to save the land. Why, then, is there all this desert?' He paused, and looked at the four Earthmen. 'And who are you? You are different: your arms and legs are thicker, your ears are small, your chests are smaller. Why?'

Platavinov explained what he could to him while he ate. Gordonov switched on the visi-screen to show the *Tovaritch* and the machines busy about her base.

'From Earth?' The Martian believed reluctantly. 'But why have you come from Earth to revive me? Why not my own people?'

It was a question which Platavinov himself would have liked to have answered. He turned it by one of his own.

'Tell me about yourself. We know practically nothing of this planet. What happened? Why were you in the state we found you?'

The Martian's story was disjointed and needed much parenthetical explanation, but later Platavinov sorted it out for the rest and translated the man's words as closely as possible.

'It happened,' said the young man, whose name, as nearly as it could be rendered, was Yauadin, 'because Mars is over-populated—was over-populated, I suppose I mean, though it seems only yesterday that we went to the hospital. All our people existed only on a narrow margin. There was no doubt that the planet had begun to wear out.

'The fertility was growing less. It was as much as we could do, by the most intensive cultivation, to produce enough food for ourselves. Then there came a year of bad harvests; our reserves soon went, and all over Mars people died of famine. The next year chanced to be better, but that was followed by another bad season, and then another.

'A great committee of investigation was called. They announced that though the three bad years were probably exceptionally severe, there could be no doubt that the productivity of the land everywhere, save close to the rivers and seas, was rapidly declining; and, further, that the rivers and seas were themselves shrinking, so that the state of affairs must inevitably become worse. In short, that Mars, in her present state, could not hope to grow enough to feed her people.

'It was a crisis too big and too easily capable of proof to be glossed over. Unless something could be done, we were facing a future of continual short rations for some, and actual starvation for the rest.

'There was a war, a bloody war of extermination in which millions were killed in order that others might live. It was a futile war, for it destroyed much of the land it was intended to preserve, and the state after it was worse than before. The fighting died away as people found that it brought them less instead of more. It became clear that nothing short of world-wide co-operation would help, and out of a great conference came the idea of the canals—the project of irrigating the whole planet from the Poles.

'At first the scheme seemed too vast to be put into practice. It was thought that such a work could never be completed, but after a time which brought forth nothing practicable save minor regional remedies, the canal idea began to be taken more seriously.

'It was accepted by many responsible people as feasible and likely to provide a solution; but it would take a very long time—centuries, perhaps—before even the main system of great canals was complete. And meanwhile the population was starving. . . .

'We were faced with a choice. Either we must go on as best we could, with our race gradually deteriorating from under-nourishment while the scheme was in hand, or else we must reduce our population in some way, so that those who remained could be properly fed. The former was scarcely feasible; the latter, at first sight, presented two possible solutions. Voluntary euthanasia for a large number of us, or, by a slower method, the deliberate limitation of births, by decree.

'It was clear that there would be few candidates for suicide in the interests of the race. But the proposal of supervised limitation aroused such passionate prejudice on all sides that it was doubtful whether the decree could ever be passed, or enforced if made law.

'It was in the middle of the inflamed arguments that the physicians put forward a new suggestion. Why not, they asked, put a large part of the race into a temporary state of suspended animation? There was almost no risk. The reduced active population, freed from the fear of hunger, could then construct the necessary machines to go forward with the canal scheme. When the system was complete and the land revived, those who had been entranced could be awakened to take up their lives again.

'Here, at last, was a plan to which in the face of our danger there could be very few objections. It was well known from many experiments that the state of suspended animation produced no harmful after-effects. In the crisis, we approved of it, and many of us actively welcomed it. To me and to my wife, Karlet, it came as the solution we had prayed for.

'We were both still young and had no wish to die of starvation, nor any other way. On the contrary, we wished very much to live and to have children of our own. But to bring them into the world to face famine, or perhaps "limitation"— which, put plainly, meant murder—at the hands of the state, was a thing we could not face.

'But here we had a gift full of new hope. We had only to submit to having our lives suspended and we would wake in a regenerated world—a world of plenty fit for our children to grow up in. We talked it over and decided to volunteer; many, many thousands like us did the same. The response was overwhelming.

'They took us as fast as the factories could turn out the containers and produce the gas. We were not the first. We had to watch many of our friends go before us, and we envied them, for every day we were forced to wait meant a day less for us in that world of plenty. But our turn came at last. I can hardly believe that it was not just a few hours ago that Karlet and I walked together to the hospital.

'And now what is there here for us? Are we to bring children into a world of deserts? Where is that world they promised us?'

He went to the window and looked out again.

'They didn't die, did they? They built the canals; that must have made the world fertile again. Why didn't they let us live in it as they had promised? Why have they cheated us and only given us deserts where you say there is not air enough to breathe?'

'They gave you nothing,' Platavinov said. 'This is a deserted city, as I told you.'

'Deserted! But there are still men on Mars?'

'Oh yes. There are some. A few thousands, I believe.'

'And they let us lie there.... Left us, meaning that we should never awake. We who volunteered to sleep so that their ancestors might live!'

He stood motionless for a long time, staring out over the waste of red sand. Platavinov watched him carefully, alert for a passionate, perhaps a dangerous reaction. But there was no sign of violence; instead, the man kept a deadening control over himself. There was fury in his eyes, but it was cold; his face grew hard and drawn. When he spoke again there was a harsh edge of bitterness on his voice.

'Tell me all you know about this place,' he demanded. 'It seems that I am a stranger in my own city—and in my own world.'

'It is easy enough to see what happened,' Platavinov told the others later. The Martian, Yauadin, was asleep in another room. He was still in need of physical rest, though the doctor had had to give him a mild sedative to calm his mind. 'Yes,' said Platavinov, 'that's clear enough.'

'Is it?' said Gordonov. 'Perhaps it is to you, but it isn't to me. What did happen?'

'Well, it looks as if this wholesale voluntary suspension of life was arranged just as he said, with perfectly honest and honourable intentions on both sides. Those who remained alive to construct the machinery to build the canals were acting in perfectly good faith, otherwise they might as well have killed these volunteers out of hand.

'But it is the old story of new generations refusing to be bound by the promises of their forefathers, As time and the irrigation work went on, life must have become easier, and with plenty for all, the population would increase. When the vast work of the canals was finished, what happened? Why, they found that the land was again supporting as many as it could; there may even have been the problem of over-population again.

'In the circumstances, how much attention would the Martians of that day be likely to pay to the promises of their great-great-grandfathers? Precious little, I'd say. To all intents and purposes, our friend Yauadin and the rest were dead. Let them stay dead, would be the verdict.

'And so, for one reason and another, it has gone on. Perhaps there has never since that day been so much surplus that it could feed several million mouths. Or perhaps by the time the surplus existed the sleepers were forgotten. Or perhaps there was no surplus until the planet began to become barren again, and then they dare not let them out.

'In any case, they were never awakened; no one ever made room for them, and now they never will. They will stay there, sealed in their containers, while the planet freezes and the Sun grows cold. It is perhaps the best thing that could happen now. They went to sleep happy, and hopeful of a new world. There will never be that new world now, but they need never know it.'

'Except Yauadin, poor chap,' said Vinski.

'He seemed to take it all pretty calmly, I thought,' Gordonov said.

'Calmly!' said Zhatkin. 'Can you see anything beyond your nose? You say he is calm—because he did not rage and swear, perhaps. You are a fool!'

Gordonov got up angrily. 'Damn you, slit-eyes! I'll teach you to call me a fool, you little——!'

Vinski swung his big bulk in between them. 'Shut up, Gordonov! And, Zhatkin, watch your tongue better.'

Zhatkin shrugged. 'No one but a fool would say that a man who seethes inside like a volcano is calm. He is not only angry; he is the most deeply angry man I have ever seen. If I were you, Vinski, I would kill him.'

All three stared at the little Kirghizian.

'What do you mean?' Vinski said.

'What I say. You should go and kill him now, while he is asleep. For two reasons. One, because it is kinder. It was cruel to bring him back to life to suffer so; it will be more cruel to let him go on suffering. And the other because he is a very, very dangerous man.'

'How, dangerous?' Platavinov wanted to know.

'I cannot say. I only know that when I see a man so tormented and cheated, and with such a look in his eyes, he is dangerous.'

'Suppose,' said Vinski, slowly. 'Suppose you go and kill him yourself.'

'I can't.'

'And nor can I.'

Zhatkin turned his dark eyes on the doctor.

'But you could, Platavinov. It is you who should give him back that peace you have taken from him. Just a matter of a little injection, and it will all be over.'

Platavinov looked hard at him. 'I don't think you know what you are suggesting, Zhatkin. It's murder, here or on Earth.'

'To rob him of his peace was a greater crime.'

'Nonsense, you're being fanciful again. I admit it has been a shock to him, a far bigger shock than I foresaw. But even so, like anyone else, he'd sooner be alive than dead. As for his being dangerous, well, I just don't understand what you mean. He's not armed; he's upset, of course, but he's no more mad than we are.'

'All right,' said Zhatkin. 'Then if you won't kill him, what do you propose to do with him—take him back to Earth with us? For I don't suppose there'll be much of a welcome for him in Hanno. Or leave him here by himself when we go?'

'We'll deal with that later. His own wishes will have to be considered.'

'I think they will.'

'I wish you wouldn't keep on hinting. What do you——?' Platavinov broke off suddenly as a bell tinkled inside the television box.

He leaned over and switched it on. The glass front glowed, and presently Soantin's face looked out at them. The doctor greeted him. The other three listened impatiently to the ensuing conversation.

'It's good news,' Platavinov told them, after he had switched off. 'The tube re-lining is almost finished. The provisioning is complete. Tomorrow they start filling the fuel tanks, and we are to be ready to leave about noon on the following day. He will tell us the exact time later.'

'Thank Lenin for that,' said Gordonov piously. 'I thought they must be pretty nearly finished—and none too early for me, either.'

'You've said it,' Vinski agreed. 'The sooner we're shooting out into space, the happier I'll feel.'

'Pity we can't have a whisky to celebrate it. I might even put up with a vodka if we had it,' Gordonov lamented.

CHAPTER EIGHT

THE REVOLT OF THE SLEEPERS

EXTERNALLY, there was nothing to distinguish the next morning from its predecessors. The Sun rose as it had risen for centuries into a featureless, cloudless sky, and shone down upon the unshaded sands. But to the Earthmen, high in their rooms in Ailiko, it had a character of its own, for it was the last day of their exile. True that it would take twelve weeks or more to cross the space which lay between them and home, but the homeward journey, once fairly begun, could no longer be considered exile. They would spend only one more night in the deserted city.

Gordonov was first into the living-room. He switched on the visi-screen, which he had left trained to the position of the *Tovaritch*, and as it cleared the sight raised his spirits still higher and banished the last trace of the doubts which had troubled him in the night.

The great rocket had already been raised to the vertical and poised on her four stabilising fins. A metal scaffolding was being erected beside it to enable the machines to reach the refuelling ports. From the open air-lock leading to the living-quarters a rope ladder hung down the shining side to the ground, 120 feet below.

Gordonov called the others in. Their eyes lit up at the sight. A delighted grin spread over Vinski's face.

'Now, at last, I can really believe that we're going to get away,' he said.

'You'd begun to doubt it?' said the doctor.

'Hadn't we all? This place seemed to take away my hope and faith in anything. The sight of the old rocket up on end again makes me feel a new man. What's wrong with you?' he added, catching sight of Zhatkin. 'Cheer up, you gloomy Tartar, we're as good as on our way now.'

'Are we? I don't feel that we are. I'm still afraid of this place.'

'Oh, all right, go on! Be a skeleton at the feast if you must, only don't rattle your bones.'

But Zhatkin's misgivings did not damp the cheerfulness of the meal with which they began the day. The sense of the deserted city outside no longer depressed their spirits, and they were full of plans. Platavinov to collect specimen instruments, a few books and pieces of minor apparatus from the hospital;

Vinski to shoot off the remainder of his films; Gordonov to make a last desperate attempt at understanding some of the machines.

Only Zhatkin put forward no plan for the day. He sat, indifferent, scarcely listening to them. At the end of the meal he asked:

'What about Yauadin? Where's he?'

'Still sleeping, I suppose,' said Platavinov. But the Kirghizian shook his head.

'He's not. I looked.'

Vinski slipped from the room. He returned in a moment.

'Zhatkin's right. He's gone! And his rug's quite cold. He must have been gone some hours.'

'Why didn't you say so before?' the doctor demanded.

Zhatkin shrugged his shoulders. 'I forgot; but it wouldn't have made any difference.'

Platavinov grunted. It was true that it would have made no difference if he had heard of it half an hour earlier, but he was irritated that Zhatkin and not himself had been the one to make the discovery.

'Anyway, he can't have gone far. He'll probably turn up for some food soon.'

Zhatkin seemed determined to make himself unpopular.

'It's perfectly obvious where he's gone,' he said, with irritating certainty.

'And where's that?'

'Why, back to where he came from. To the vaults under the hospital, of course.'

Gordonov got up and went to the cupboard where they kept the space-suits. There were only three there; the one he himself had been using had gone.

Vinski rose. 'We'd better go after him. The poor devil will go crazy alone in that place. After all, we owe him something for what we've done to him. We might even take him back to Earth, if there's no other way of dealing with him. Get another suit out of the stores and come along to the hospital, Gordonov.'

All four made their way through the underground passage together. At the hospital lock, Platavinov pushed over the opening lever, but the door remained closed.

'That's odd,' he said. 'It's never failed before.' He tried again, but the door still refused to move.

'Better try the ground-level entrance,' Vinski suggested.

They went back a little and gained the surface by way of the nearest empty building. The main entrance-lock of the hospital faced them as they emerged. Again Platavinov pulled over a lever which should have admitted them, but like the other, the door failed to respond.

'He's jiggered the works somehow,' said Gordonov. 'Seems as if he didn't want us.'

Vinski agreed. 'And I don't see that there's much we can do about it,' he added.

'That's all very well,' protested Platavinov, looking round from a further assault on the door. 'But if I can't get in, I can't get hold of those instruments and specimens. There must be other ways into the place.'

'One perhaps, but certainly not many,' Vinski said. 'The less entrances, the less loss of their precious air.'

'I've got to get in somehow,' muttered Platavinov, grimly.

The other three helped for a time in the search for another entrance, but as the Sun rose higher they left him to find it for himself. Vinski was unwilling to waste his last chances of taking photographs, and Gordonov was anxious to make his last bid for understanding the machines in the workshops. It would be hard luck for Platavinov if he could not collect the specimens to take back to Earth, but it was not sense for them all to waste time on the one job.

Zhatkin, with a characteristic shrug, drifted off too. He made his way back to their living-room and settled down at the control panel of the visi-screen. He tuned it first to show the busy streets of Hanno—streets which were thronged with moving crowds, not of men, but of shining machines. Only rarely did he catch a glimpse of a helmeted human figure in its space-suit.

The machines interested him deeply. He found it easier than his companions to believe that they were sentient, and he wanted very much to know the degree of self-control to which they had attained. Still more he wanted to know how they were built. It irked him extremely that whenever he set the focus for the inside of one of the factories, the screen went blank, just as it did when he tried to look inside any of the other buildings.

The best that he could do was to adjust his view-point so that it was just outside the factory doors, but that was unsatisfactory, too; the view was limited, and half the time it was obliterated by machines passing in and out.

One thing his observations of Hanno had told him was that whatever the relationship between the men and the machines, the former certainly did not exercise direct control, and that if the city contained a human population of only some 3,000, as Soantin had said, the machines must outnumber them a good many to one.

When he tired of that, he tried to explore another interest. Raising his view-point to some thousand feet above ground level, he set out to follow the great canal which led southward from Hanno. One day he had seen something ploughing slowly through its waters. Whether it had been creature or machine he did not know, for in the effort to get a closer view he had muddled his controls and lost it altogether.

He would have liked to know for certain whether animal life on such a scale had managed to survive in the Martian waters, or if he had chanced to get a glimpse of a commercial vessel still plying between the few surviving cities. But miles of the canal moved in a broad ribbon across the screen, and left him unrewarded.

The day wore on. No one came to disturb Zhatkin as he sat flitting the visi-screen hither and thither across the half-planet which was its range. Doubtless the others had come back to the building in the course of the day to exchange their depleted oxygen packs for fully-charged ones, but they had not come upstairs. He was glad of that. He had no wish to talk to them. He was quite content to sit and, a little sadly, watch the scenes pass before him.

A sense which he did not attempt to analyse told him that he could do nothing useful. It was something of the same feeling which had come upon him when he suggested that Yauadin should be killed. . . .

The Sun was only an hour or two off setting when a sound of feet in the passage brought him out of his contemplations. He turned to see Gordonov enter—Gordonov, and a stranger, both in space-suits. One of the engineer's hands was firmly clamped on his companion's arm.

'Platavinov here?' he asked. 'I want to hear what this chap has to say.'

He thrust the other man into the room and, taking up a tactical position near the door, removed his helmet.

Zhatkin looked curiously at the newcomer. He was undoubtedly a Martian, and his features were set similarly to Yauadin's. The man seated himself on the divan, with an air of great weariness, and, seeing that it was safe to do so, unfastened his helmet and dropped it to the floor. He sat for some seconds with his face in his hands. As he looked up again, his eyes met Zhatkin's and he said something in his own language.

Zhatkin could not understand the words, but he had seen a worn out, exhausted man before. He led him over to the switchboard and pressed a lever. The Martian understood what was expected of him. He spoke a few words into the diaphragm, and a few minutes later he was making a meal with the intensity of a desperately hungry man.

'Where did you come across him?' Zhatkin asked Gordonov.

'Spotted him slinking around in one of the engineering shops. Thought it was that fellow Yauadin at first, but it isn't.'

'So I see. But who is it?'

'That's what I want to know. I brought him along for Platavinov to find out. He came quietly enough. Not much strength in these chaps, anyway, by the skinny look of 'em; and this one seems pretty well all in. What I don't understand——'

He broke off as Vinski entered hurriedly.

'There's something queer happening! I swear I saw a couple of men in one of the streets just now. It—— Who's that?' he asked abruptly, as he caught sight of the stranger. 'Where did he come from? What's going on?'

'I don't think it's too difficult to guess,' said Zhatkin, thoughtfully.

Platavinov arrived a few minutes later in a state of great agitation.

'He's done it! By Lenin, you were right, Zhatkin! We should never have let him go. He's waking them. There are lights in the hospital; people moving inside. What do you think they'll do?'

'Better ask this one,' Gordonov advised, bringing forward his capture.

Platavinov, swinging round at the Martian, fired a series of rapid questions at him. The other did not answer at once. The food had done him good, giving him new strength, but it had not taken the lines from his face. He stood looking steadily into the doctor's eyes. Then he began to speak slowly, distinctly, and with a malevolence which no one could misunderstand.

Platavinov was clearly taken aback by the venom in his voice, but in a few seconds his expression of amazement gave place to one of understanding. He interjected a swift sentence, and the Martian's manner, too, underwent a change. Vinski and the others were obliged to wait impatiently through a considerable conversation until Platavinov turned to give them the gist of it. He looked worried as he did so.

'He thought at first that we were Martians,' he explained.

'He calmed off a bit when I told him who we really are, but it seems to me as if there is going to be trouble.

'It was Yauadin who brought this off, all right. He left here some time during the night, and went straight to the hospital. There he found the machinery for aeration and set it going. He guessed that we might follow him, and put all the entrances to the place out of action. The moment there was sufficient pressure of air, he set about opening the containers and bringing his friends back to life.

'As soon as the first had recovered enough, they joined in and helped him. They've been at it fourteen hours now, and there are hundreds of them out already. They've been able to bring them round quicker than I could; all the necessary stuff is to hand in the hospital. They're still at it now, as hard as they can go!'

'What are they going to do?' Vinski asked.

'First, they are going to put this city in full working order again; this chap and some others have been looking round with an eye to getting things going. Then they're going all out to revenge themselves on the existing cities. They mean to wipe out any Martians who still exist.

'You heard that fellow's tone when he thought we were Martians. That's how they feel about them. It's going to be no half-hearted business once they get going!'

'But can they do it? Make the city work again, I mean? And will it be possible for them to make enough synthetic food to keep going? They'll need raw materials of some kind for that,' said Gordonov.

'I can't say. I don't suppose they can yet, either. In any case, they probably wouldn't care. Why should they? It gives them a chance to live for a while, at any rate; nothing else does. Above everything else, they're mad with the idea of revenge— of wiping out the people who failed them and left them to lie there. That's what matters most to them now. It's a kind of holy war to them. Tomorrow they're going to send men out to start opening the containers in other cities.'

'But how many are there? There must be millions altogether. The place can't possibly support them.'

'I know; but they're desperate, don't you understand? Besides, Yauadin has told them about us. He has said that if it is possible for us to cross space, it is possible for them. They will build rockets as soon as they can, and colonise on Earth or Venus. Somehow or other, they intend to have the life that was promised to them.

'But before everything else they intend that their own

people shall pay the price for cheating them. And they'll make sure that it's paid, too! We've seen how two men feel about it. Imagine a thousand—a hundred thousand—in the same frame of mind. . . .'

CHAPTER NINE

JOURNEY'S END

VINSKI nodded. If all the men and women released were capable of such cold, bitter fury as those two, there would be no quarter for the inhabitants of Hanno and the other cities.

'We'd better warn Soantin,' he said. 'We can't just stand by and let these people get ready to wipe him and his lot out.'

Gordonov agreed. 'He could send the machines against them and make sure that no more of the containers are opened. Perhaps they'll be able to support those who are free already.'

'That's no good.' Platavinov shook his head. 'I told this man that they would find thousands of the machines to deal with in Hanno. It didn't worry him. They know how the machines work. They can paralyse them, he said. I don't see that there's anything to be done.'

'Well, at least we can warn Soantin,' Vinski repeated. 'We must. We owe our lives to him; the least we can do is to let him know what is happening. After all, we're responsible for it happening at all.'

'That's just it,' said Platavinov. 'We are responsible—at least, I am. And how is he going to feel about that?'

'It was unintentional. We could not foresee what would follow when you had revived the man. We had not even been warned. He can't blame us over-much; but in any case it is our duty to warn him before things go any farther.' Vinski's opinion was quite definite. Gordonov backed him up.

'It may still be possible for him to take steps now which he could not take later,' he said.

'And you, Zhatkin?' the doctor asked.

Zhatkin raised his musing eyes. 'Yes, that would be best, I think. Though I doubt its use; I fancy the damage is done now.'

Platavinov thought for a moment before he directed Gordonov to take the Martian away and lock him up in one of the other rooms.

By the time the engineer returned, Soantin's face was visible on the screen of the television-box. Platavinov was leaning forward, speaking rapidly and intensely in the Martian tongue. Soantin's expression became more serious. He asked several questions which the doctor answered without hesitation. There was a look of decision upon his face as the conversation came to an end and the picture faded.

'Well?' asked Vinski.

'I don't think it is quite as serious as we feared. He is going to send the machines against them and stop the opening of further containers until it has been decided what is to be done with the already revived. He says that they are mistaken about the machines, for the method of powering them was not discovered until centuries after the containers were sealed.

'He does not blame us, for he understands that we acted in ignorance, but he thinks it will be best to get us out of the way as soon as possible. The *Tovaritch* refuelling is almost finished now, and he is giving orders for the inclination to be altered so that we can take off six hours earlier; he can't make it sooner than that.'

'That will make it soon after dawn,' said Gordonov. 'Why shouldn't we go aboard now and sleep there?'

'Partly because the refuelling is not yet quite complete, and partly because there is not at present any air in the living-room. They have to finish connecting up the fresh oxygen tanks.'

'And he is sure he can look after the other business?' Vinski asked.

'He hasn't any doubt about it. A few hundred of the machines can easily handle the situation, he says. So we don't seem to have done so much damage as we feared after all,' Platavinov said with satisfaction.

'Now as to tomorrow——' he went on, but Zhatkin's voice cut him short.

'Platavinov,' he said, slowly and distinctly, 'why are you lying?'

The doctor swung round, fists clenched, and glared down upon the smaller man. Zhatkin, without moving from his seat on the divan, looked calmly into the other's angry face.

'What do you mean?' Platavinov shouted. 'You little rat of a Tartar, I'll——!'

Vinski intervened, pushing the doctor aside. To Zhatkin he said:

'What's all this about? Why did you say he was a liar?'

Zhatkin shrugged. 'Because he is a liar. He never mentioned

the containers, or the people in them, to Soantin just now.'

Platavinov's jaw dropped. One glance at him was enough to show that the thrust had gone home. He recovered himself, but too late.

'You don't know what I said or did not say. You can't understand a word of their language.'

'No?' said Zhatkin, softly.

Platavinov looked away. 'Well, what if I didn't tell him? If there's going to be trouble here, isn't it better for all of us to get away as soon as we can before it starts? It's not our affair, and there's no reason why we should be mixed up in it. The sooner we get out, the better; that's why I got him to advance the starting time.'

'Oh, then that part's true?' said Gordonov.

'Of course it is! But if you're still fools enough to want Soantin to know about the rest before he must, you'd better get Zhatkin to tell him—for I won't.'

Zhatkin shook his head. 'Unfortunately, I can't. I didn't need to; you told the lies in our own language.'

'In that case,' said Platavinov, 'it seems that Soantin is going to remain uninformed.'

They rose next morning by the first light. Platavinov spoke into the microphone, ordering the last food they would eat on Mars. Gordonov switched on the visi-screen and focused it once more on the *Tovaritch*. It cleared, and showed the rocket ready for the take-off, with the morning sun reflecting brightly from her polished hull. The effect of the doctor's talk with Soantin was noticeable at once, for the whole ship was now tilted several degrees to the left, and the rope ladder which had laid against the side now hung free for the greater part of its length.

All four rose to look at it. It seemed too long expected to be true that they were ready to go at last. In less than an hour now they would be back in the familiar living-room, making themselves comfortable on their couches for the start. In just over an hour they would be out in space, well started on their three months' fall from planet to planet.

Vinski, to save wasting time later on, was already pulling on his silvery space-suit ready for the walk to the rocket. The others followed his example.

The last meal finished, they set about gathering together their belongings and such specimens as they had decided to take back to Earth. Vinski was decorating himself with his film cameras and pulling out of a cupboard the rifles which had proved a needless precaution. Platavinov was packing together the objects he had acquired before the closing of the hospital, including the flask of green gas taken from Yauadin's container.

Gordonov had a small motor which would, he hoped, be the means of supplying the world with an entirely new form of power once he could find anybody able to make head or tail of it. He was improvising a cord sling which would enable him to take it up the rope ladder. Only Zhatkin, it seemed, had nothing to take from Mars but what he had brought. He sat unexcitedly watching the others.

Vinski straightened himself and looked round the room. 'Is there anything——?' he had begun, when a sound of running footsteps made him break off.

Yauadin, wearing a space-suit, but helmetless like themselves, appeared in the doorway. For a moment he looked at them. Then he singled Platavinov out from the rest. There was a look of vivid fury on his face; the semi-control he had shown before had gone, the hatred in his eyes was limitless. Platavinov stepped back involuntarily.

A flood of words broke from the Martian. Harsh, bitter-toned phrases, delivered as if they were blows. The doctor stepped back again, raising his hand as though to ward the other off. But the Martian came no nearer. Platavinov seemed utterly confounded. Once he started to expostulate in a fumbling way, but the other talked him down.

The climax came too suddenly for the rest to suspect it. Yauadin raised his right arm and pointed it at the man before him. Vinski, with immense presence of mind, flung himself upon him. But he was too late. The instant before he reached him there was a searing, soundless flash, and as the two men crashed over together, Platavinov slithered down the wall, a hole burnt through his head.

The silence that followed lasted only a few seconds. It was broken by a shout from Gordonov.

'Look! Vinski, look!'

He was pointing to the visi-screen. Three figures in silver space-suits were climbing the swaying ladder up the *Tovaritch*'s side. One stood in the open doorway above, four more on the ground at the foot of the ladder.

Vinski took in the scene at a glance. With a bound he was across the room and had snatched up his helmet.

'Come on,' he shouted to the others, as he made for the doorway. Gordonov, helmet also in hand, was only a few steps behind him.

Zhatkin did not move.

He remained sitting on the edge of the divan, looking at the bodies of the two men. They were both beyond hope. There was a hole right through Platavinov's head; Yauadin's head had cracked on the floor as he went down under Vinski's weight.

He needed no explanation of what had occurred. More than once among the Martian's invective he had caught the word 'Karlet.' Karlet, Platavinov had told them, was the name of Yauadin's wife, with whom he had gone so hopefully to the hospital on that day so many centuries ago.

What could be more natural than that husband and wife should have laid in their containers side by side? And after that unfortunate opening of the first container—that 'accident,' as Platavinov had called it—they had taken the next one to it to bring back here. It was Karlet who had died in that vault, and her body had been there for Yauadin to find. . . .

Zhatkin looked across at the broken body. Well, at least the unhappy, twice-embittered Yauadin had peace now.

He looked back once more to the visi-screen. The last of the space-suited figures was nearing the top of the ladder now. A movement in the lower right-hand corner of the scene caught his eye. Two human figures accompanied by several scuttering machines were racing towards the rocket-ship.

Suddenly, a moment after he had noticed them, the machines came to a dead stop and froze motionless. But the two human beings kept on. Though they were too small for him to distinguish details, he knew that they were Vinski and Gordonov by the superhuman strides in which their Earthly muscles carried them over the sand.

One running figure reached the dangling ladder a little ahead of the other. He leapt at it, and began to climb like a monkey. The other was only a yard or two behind him.

The last of the earlier climbers was in the air-lock now. Zhatkin saw him lean out and look down at the two Earthmen. Already the leader was halfway up the ladder. Then the man in the air-lock bent down. Another moment, and ladder and climbers fell together to the ground. The outer door of the air-lock closed.

Of the climbers, one—it was impossible to say which—lay where he had fallen among the loops of the ladder. The other jumped to his feet and gazed up at the towering rocket, shaking both his fists at it in impotent frenzy. It was some minutes before he noticed his companion's plight. When he did, he went over and lifted the other man's head.

Even at the size they were on the screen, it was clear that the helmet was smashed. Asphyxiation, if not the fall, had finished the journey for him. Slowly the survivor straightened up. Once more he looked long and steadily up the shimmering side of the rocket. Then he picked up his fallen companion and began to plod with a slow, weary step back towards the city.

There came a sudden burst of flame, fierce as a part of the Sun itself, between the flanges of the rocket. Zhatkin drew back with his hand over his smarting eyes. When he was able to look again the *Tovaritch* had gone. Where she had stood was a pit of fused and blackened sand. Of the man who had been carrying the other back there was no sign. . . .

Zhatkin sat awhile without moving. Then he sighed. His sad eyes searched slowly round the room, loitered for a space on the rifles which Vinski had dropped as he sprang at the Martian, passed on to Platavinov's body, and then to Yauadin's.

What would happen? he wondered. Would the *Tovaritch* make the journey back to Earth with her Martian crew? Or to Venus, perhaps? Or would she be lost for ever in the depths of space? He would never know.

He found himself staring at an object which lay close beside Yauadin. It looked something like an electric torch, save that it was open at the end where the glass should be. He walked slowly across and picked it up. A simple-looking little weapon, but effective, as Yauadin had shown. Apparently one operated it by pressing a neat little knob on the side.

Zhatkin looked round the room once more. He sighed again. Then he put the tube against his head and pressed the little knob.

WORLDS TO BARTER

CHAPTER ONE

THE REFUGEE FROM 2145

OUTSIDE the tall laboratory windows, the Sun shone brightly on the gardens. It was that kind of June morning when one forgets the deficiencies of our civilisation and everything seems for the best, in the best of all possible worlds. Certainly, in the minds of Professor Lestrange and myself there was no suspicion of any untoward occurrence. We had already been working for some three and a half severely practical hours.

Lestrange, in that year 1945, was not unlike the photographs, taken ten years later, which now adorn the text-books. Already, at forty, his most striking characteristics were that broad, white forehead where so many mysteries were solved, and those piercing eyes which saw so much that was hidden from ordinary men. Already his adaptations and improvements marked him for success, though he had made none of those revolutionary discoveries individual enough to be understood and acclaimed by the public. The time was yet to come when the name of Lestrange would be more familiar than that of Edison had ever been, and when his commanding face would peer out from a million printed pages.

The critical moments of our present experiment were approaching. I was attempting to fight down my rising excitement so that no trembling might show in my hands. Lestrange was, to all appearances, as calm as a frozen sea. During his work, he preserved the mien of a poker player. Not a hurried movement betrayed any anxiety as, in the silence of the long laboratory, he tested the last connections and inspected the final adjustments.

'Stand by,' he ordered at length, in an unemotional voice.

As I moved aside, his hand was on the switch. My eyes were fixed upon the intricate apparatus before us. In a few seconds, now, the throw of a copper bar would prove whether we faced a marvellous discovery or the symbol of wasted months of labour. Suddenly, there was a mighty crash behind us.

That noise, so dreaded in our surroundings, hit my taut nerves like a hundred volts. I whirled round. Lestrange's scientific abstraction was shattered. Slowly his hand left the switch, and his mouth dropped open. At any other time, the way blank amazement succeeded intelligent concentration might have amused me, but now, I myself was too bewildered.

Two-thirds of the way up the room, in the middle of what had been a clear floor space, lay a piece of machinery. A few feet from it sprawled the figure of a man.

As we stared, the man sat up. He was dressed in a close-fitting, black suit of a texture and finish resembling leather, and apparently made in one piece. His build was tall and strong, and his face, though it bore an expression of confusion at the moment, showed firmness of character.

For a few seconds he gazed about, wonderingly, then alarm seized him. His voice was urgent as he addressed us.

'Quick!' he said. 'Some string. Quick!'

Something in his manner caused me to search my pockets without question. 'Here,' I said, holding out a length of packing twine.

He snatched it, and turned to the machine behind him. Hurriedly, he raised the contraption from its side to a vertical position. More than anything else, it seemed to resemble the skeleton framework of a miniature building using, instead of steel, bright silvery bars which criss-crossed in all directions. Enmeshed in them was a bucket seat, before which were arrayed two rows of dials. There was no time for a further examination.

The stranger leaned over the instrument board, adjusted several dials, tied a loop in the end of my bit of string and slipped it over a small lever. He took as many steps away as the length of the string permitted, and gave a jerky pull. . . .

There was no machine; before our startled eyes stood only the stranger, the string dangling from his hand. A sigh of relief broke from his lips as he turned towards us.

'Gentlemen,' he said, 'I owe you an apology.'

'You do, sir,' replied Lestrange. 'I should be pleased to know by what right you intrude.'

'I admit, I have no right. I can plead only what they used to call in the old days, sanctuary. You are Mr. Lestrange—the inventor of the battery? My own name is Lestrange—Jon Lestrange.'

'My name is Lestrange,' the Professor admitted, 'but I have invented no battery.'

'Not yet?' said the stranger. 'I am earlier than I thought. You must excuse me, my dates were never good.'

There was puzzlement on Lestrange's face as he replied. 'I do not understand you. No doubt you will explain later. Meanwhile, am I to infer from your name that you claim relationship?'

'Certainly we are related, but—er—distantly.'

'The matter must be examined. I cannot pretend ever to have heard of you before. Let me present my assistant, Harry Wright.'

The stranger held out his hand. 'I've heard of you, Mr. Wright,' he said with a smile. 'Your rescue of Mr. Lestrange was an act of real bravery.'

It was my turn to be puzzled. In all the six years I had known Lestrange, he had never been in more danger than anyone who crosses a busy street.

'I see I have made another blunder. Please forgive me,' the man apologised. Then a change came over his expression. The smile of greeting gave way to a look of anguish. His eyes seemed to plead as he asked:

'Tell me, have you ever, either of you, seen or heard of another machine like the one I came on?'

We shook our heads. I could recall no invention bearing any resemblance to it.

'There was really no chance; not one in a hundred million,' he said slowly. 'I knew it wasn't possible, but I had to ask.'

His gaze wandered round the room, pausing here and there upon apparatus, until it came to rest upon the material of our thwarted experiment. His eyes brightened, and he took a few steps towards it.

Lestrange and I were recovering, now, from our sense of unreality. Our eyes met, and we knew that the same thought was in both our minds. All mystery was ripped from the affair with a jerk—the man was a spy. With the minutest care, he was examining the product of our secret months of labour. Lestrange pulled a revolver from a drawer.

'Put your hands up!' he snapped. The other obeyed, a slight smile on his lips.

'I've heard that these were troublous times,' he remarked.

'Come over here,' Lestrange ordered, 'and tell us just why you are so interested in that experiment.'

The other, who called himself Lestrange, opened his eyes wide in evident surprise.

'Surely,' he expostulated, 'it is reasonable to show interest in the discovery which changed the face of the world? Besides, I may be mistaken, but it seems slightly different from what I remember. It's a couple of years since I saw a picture of it, but

I have a distinct impression that several of the connections ran differently ... that terminal on the left should be coupled direct to——'

'What on earth are you talking about?' roared Lestrange. 'You must be mad! The thing's only been assembled four days.'

'Oh, Lord,' said the stranger, 'I've put my foot in it again. I'll have to try to explain it all to you—but it's a long story. May I have some food first? I haven't eaten for twenty-four hours.'

By the end of the meal, the visitor's status had changed. He was no longer an interloper, but a guest whom we were calling, at his own request, Jon. Somehow, in that desultory form of conversation appropriate to the lunch table, we had lost our suspicions, though we were no nearer to understanding him. He was curiously ignorant at the same time that he was well-informed. His broad outlines of current politics were good, but of the details he seemed to know nothing.

In speaking of well-known characters, he appeared to hesitate, as though he might commit himself. His knowledge of literature was excellent, though occasionally he referred to works of which I had never heard, by authors whose fame was world-wide. My condensed impression was that, while he appreciated the high-lights of most matters, he was sure of himself only in a few subjects.

'You'll smoke?' inquired Lestrange, as we retired to his comfortable study.

'Tobacco?' asked Jon.

'Of course,' replied the Professor, with a touch of surprise. 'What else?'

'There are many things to smoke where I come from—one has to be careful.'

He settled himself comfortably in a big chair and lit a cigar.

'Now,' he said, 'if you can put up with a long tale, I would like to explain this intrusion.'

'Our experiment...' I began.

'Would not be a success in its present form. Believe me, I can tell you where there is a miscalculation.'

I accepted his statement. He seemed to know something of our work. Lestrange, too, nodded agreement.

John began:

'I think the first thing to be explained is why I chose to thrust my company upon you rather than upon anyone else. Perhaps the first reason is our relationship, and the second that my studies have informed me that you, Professor, have probably a more open mind and a greater grasp of possibilities than any man now living. . . .'

'This relationship . . .?'

'Our family has been proud of its direct descent from you and your wife, Joy.'

Lestrange and I looked at one another. Now, there was no doubt that the man was off the rails somewhere.

'But I'm not married. I——'

'Please let me go my own way. It is a difficult situation, but I hope I shall convince you. Very few men can have had the chance of convincing their great-great-great grandfathers of anything. . . . But I am now an anachronism. You see, I was born in the year A.D. 2118—or should it be, I *shall be* born in 2118?—and I am—or will be—a refugee from the twenty-second century. I assure you that you will be married shortly, but I can't remember when—I think I told you I was not very good at dates.

'It will probably be easier for you if I tell you the story in the past tense. Certainly, it is a past life for me. You saw me burn my bridges when I tied the string to that machine. . . .

'Of the nature of time, we of the twenty-second century knew little more than you of the twentieth. Habit of thought still caused us still to think of it in terms of progression along a straight line. We were aware, of course, that this was inaccurate, yet for all practical purposes it serves us as well as it had served the world for thousands of years before.

'Because I am here now, I know that time is somehow folded or circular so that it is all co-existent, or non-existent; but of the working principle of that machine which brought me here, I am as ignorant as you. I set the dials, pulled the lever—and there was your laboratory. And I daren't keep the thing to examine it. It's almost certain that the owners had some way of tracing it, and that wasn't a risk worth taking.

CHAPTER TWO

A VOICE FROM THE FUTURE

'THE world I was living in was not all you twentieth-century men expected. It would have disappointed Wells and his fellow prophets to have had a true vision of A.D. 2145. We were on another swing of the pendulum. Scientific progress in the sense of physics, chemistry and engineering, had slowed its advance to a minimum while the world caught up and re-adjusted. By the end of the twentieth century science was so far advanced that civilisation was becoming seriously lopsided, so that nature tended to restore the balance.

'Even today I expect you can begin to see how large-scale production has begun to upset politics and social conditions which were designed to cope with a simpler way of life. It is making war no longer the solution of difficulties; it is uprooting the old order of things but not reorganising. So you will see that I come from a world in which Mr. Wells' "Sleeper" might awake, but from an age which had spent the previous century improving its institutions rather than its machines.

'Since the year 2000 the Lestrange battery, of which you have heard me speak, had been almost the only driving agent for machinery. In 2000, Mr. Lestrange, the internal combustion engine will have passed away. The whole world's trains, ships, planes, radios, cranes, everything save the most ponderous machines will be depending upon your discovery.

'It is strange to tell a man of his results before the experiment has been made. Nevertheless I assure you that your little storage battery is going to have a greater effect upon the whole world than any other single invention in the history of mankind. Even the machine which brought me here depended upon a modified form of your battery to carry it across half a million years.'

'But you said——'

'Oh, yes, I have taken only a little local trip on it. A mere jaunt of a couple of centuries. . . .

'Looking back, I can see that the first sign of the crisis we were to face occurred about a year ago—to me—in the summer of 2144. An account was published, by newspapers and radio, of the derailing of a train—it was still more economical for heavy, imperishable goods to be carried by rail. An investigation of the accident, so far from clearing up the reason, had obscured it.

'Among the débris was found the crooked frame of what we later learned to call a "time-traveller." Attention was first attracted to the silvery bars by their strength: though the joints of the structure had been strained by the impact, rods a quarter of an inch thick were found to be supporting tons of wreckage without a bend. This unknown, silvery metal itself set a problem, but a greater puzzle was the body found lying near the track.

'There could be no doubt that the corpse was human,

though to us, whose standards were still those of ancient Greece, the thing appeared a travesty. In height, it must have stood about five feet. The head had twice the volume of ours, though the enlargement was mainly frontal. The neck was thickened to support the weight, until the shoulders barely projected. Puny arms ended in small hands, of which no finger carried a nail and none was longer than two inches. Each foot was just a pad showing no articulation of the toes.

'When the dissectors got to work on the body, they noticed many other curious malformations, such as abbreviated intestines, an atrophied aural system and absence of teeth. Speculation ran rife. Everyone made the creature's origin a sort of guessing game. It was suggested that the thing was a natural freak, a product of vivisectional experiment, a sensational hoax, an attempt at artificial creation and a dozen other things all equally wide of the mark.

'The only explanation which attempted to account for the machine was offered by an ingenious gentleman who claimed that the body was that of an interplanetary explorer who had selected a singularly unfortunate spot for his landing. It was curtly pointed out that a metal framework is not the best protection against a vacuum. It nevertheless transpired, later, that the only thing seriously wrong with this explanation was the inclusion of the word "interplanetary."

'As the controversy began to cool, it suddenly received fresh fuel from the finding of a similar body in a coastal rock-pool. The boy who reported it said there had been a shiny machine near, but when he touched a lever, it had disappeared. Again the crop of surmise sprouted. Every suggestion which could be made, was made; save the right one—that the people of 2144 had gazed on the bodies of their own remote descendants. But could we have read in the mystery the warning it carried, it would have been useless to us.

'Three months ago, the curtain rose on the last act of our drama—only three months.'

Jon paused, and looked at us with bitterness in his eyes.

'Then,' he said, 'it was a happy world. A civilisation progressing serenely, as it thought, to its appointed goal. Now, it is swept away. All time and space are warped, distorted and incomprehensible. . . .

'It was my happiest night. A dream had started its flow towards reality—now Fate has ordained that the dream remains a dream. Somewhere in the intricate tissues of time, Mary may still live, but the dream can never be fulfilled, now.

'Across that evening, which surely was made for lovers to plan their future, clashed the voice of our doom. Over the whole broadcast belt, in all the world, those unemotional tones were heard.

' "People of the Twenty-Second Century," the voice began. "We of the five thousand and twenty-second century offer peace. We come from a period in the world's history which holds no hope for us. We have conquered time that we may gain the Earth. We offer two kinds of peace: one is elimination, the other, submission to our will.

' "We are not cruel. We do not wish to kill you, our ancestors. Instead, we give transportation—you will exchange your world for ours. We will carry you across the gulf of half a million years to a world in which you, a short-lived race, will be well suited, as will your sons and your sons' sons. For us who count our years by thousands as you count by tens, the end is too near. We have broken through time that we may continue our work. Prepare yourselves and your possessions, that you may be ready for the time and places we shall appoint."

'Neither Mary nor I knew what to make of it—indeed, we heard it only subconsciously. Tomorrow would explain. Tonight, we had more important matters to discuss.

'The next day did not explain; it only complicated. Where did the voice originate? How had it compassed all wavelengths? How was it of equal strength at antipodes? Why did no picture of the speaker come through on the television screens? It caused a vague uneasiness. Though no one understood nor took much interest in the message itself, the curious form of transmission was disturbing to a world unused to new inventions.

'The general attitude of science had resulted in the feeling that things were very well as they stood and that tamperers should be put down with a firm hand. Even the type who immediately attributes the incomprehensible to a form of practical joke felt that easy solution to be inadequate. The mass of the people wondered unintelligently, suggesting hazily that "something ought to be done about it." Governments officially disregarded it, and privately, did not know what to make of it.

'A few days later came the second world-wide call. Mary and I were sitting at the open window when the voice made us jump round.

' "But I shut the radio off," said Mary in surprise.

'I crossed the room and inspected the switches. Undoubted-

ly, they were out—though there might be a short somewhere. I pulled the leads from the speaker, and then stared at
the thing in amazement, for the voice still continued:

'"... seems, in view of the fact that no preparations have
been made, that you have not understood our intentions...."

'It was uncanny. I picked up the speaker and carried it across
the room. I know a few tricks to make an unattached speaker
work, but none of them was being used here. The voice went
on:

'"... not our wish to hurt anyone, but such as do not accede
to our demands must be eliminated. It is suggested that, for
the purpose of convincing yourselves that this is no empty
threat, a committee shall be appointed to visit us and report
its findings to the world. Thus you shall be convinced that
obedience to our will is the only course not leading to elimination. This committee will gather at the Paris Air Station,
whence we will provide a means of travel one week from today
at exactly this hour."

'I looked at Mary, and she at me. There was trouble in our
eyes. There was something behind that unemotional voice
which told us that this affair was far from a practical joke.
Feeling, not reason, told us it was serious.

'"I am going on that committee," I said at last. "Somehow
or other, I'll join it and find out what's at the bottom of all
this."

'Mary nodded. "Good, Jon; that's like you," she approved.
Then a little frown appeared. "You don't think it's dangerous?"

'"Not a bit," I assured her. "There'd be no point in assemb-
ling a committee just to kill its members—or 'eliminate' them,
as the voice puts it. They might just as well start 'eliminating'
right away. No; I think, who ever they are, they're on the
square, and though the whole show sounds insane, there's
something pretty big behind it."

'Far below, we had seen the coast of France slip away from
beneath our queer craft. Now, through the thick glass windows, the blue waves of the Mediterranean twinkled at us.
Around me, as I gazed down, buzzed the tentative suggestions
of a puzzled committee.

'Such influence as I possessed had been exerted with successful results. A large air liner had carried me rapidly from home
to drop our gliding tender at Le Bourget, the Paris airport.
There I had found a group awaiting the craft promised by the

radio voice. It was a cosmopolitan collection of Americans, Germans, English, French, Japanese, Chinese, Indian and most other nationalities.

'Not one of them officially represented his government. The rulers assumed an ignorance of the ultimatum; nevertheless, they had assisted brilliant men to attend. The unknown had managed to infuse into his short speeches some quality which attracted many intellectuals.

'I had left myself a narrow margin, for within an hour of my arrival our craft was sighted. At a great height the watchers saw a silver cylinder hurling itself towards us. At that moment, I believe, some began to realise the possibility of a menace. All eyes gazed up.

'Only random guesses as to the size of the craft could be made at such a distance, but as it drew nearer we judged it to be about equal to one of our larger airships. Built of silvery metal, it tapered at each end, and along the sides were rows of windows. Nothing more was to be seen; it gave no clue to the manner of the propulsion.

'Suddenly from all the loudspeakers, both in the control tower and around the ground, snapped the one word: "Landing." The ground crew rushed for the lighter-than-air machines hurriedly assembled, and then found that there was nothing for them to do. Down and down the great cylinder dropped, to land as lightly as a leaf.

' "The Committee will come aboard," said the voice we were beginning to know so well. Simultaneously, sections of the hull opened outwards, the hinges being at the bottom, so that the doors themselves formed ramps.

'For a moment, we looked at one another in hesitation, then we stepped forward as though by common consent. There was no one to welcome us on board. Into a great saloon, seemingly the full length of the ship, we flocked. With a click, the doors closed and we were off to heaven knew where. Thousands of feet above the ordinary traffic levels, we turned and sped to the south.

'After the first surprise of departure had worn off, we found our tongues again. It seemed as though most of us found them at the same moment.

' "I do not like this affair; not at all—no!" said a little Frenchman whom I recognised as M. Duvain of the French Air Roads. "It is all too mysterious. Are we children that they make to us the effect of the stage thrill? It is a bad begin, such nonsense, for the serious investigation, no?"

' "Damn ridiculous, the whole thing," replied Sir Henry

Deen, standing near. "Silly scare by some jokers, in my opinion. However, they're in for it now. We'll soon show 'em what's what!"

'The Frenchman nodded his agreement. "And you, m'sieur," he said, turning to me. "Do you not think it is an insult to treat a so distinguished party as a flock of sheep? No reception, no speeches?"

' "If it is a practical joke," I suggested, "you don't want to be made more of a fool, do you?"

' "Then you, too, think that it may be a practical joke?" asked Sir Henry. I informed him that I had come to observe and to draw conclusions from those observations. I had no intention of muddling myself by prejudice, nor of building theories without foundation. Not a polite answer, but the pair irritated me.

' "The desert!" shouted someone. I turned back to the window, and saw that we were heading over miles of rolling sands towards the heart of the Sahara.

CHAPTER THREE

THE SENILE WORLD

'THREE quarters of an hour later, the familiar voice gave its laconic "Landing." Below us lay a building. It was shorter than the craft we were in; some three hundred feet by one hundred and fifty, and rising about sixty. The whole place was entirely constructed of the silvery metal.

'The ship settled without a jar. The doors fell open and we walked out, to find ourselves face to face with a seamless, shining wall, in which one patch of darkness framed a waiting figure.

'Exclamations of surprise rose from the party. There can hardly have been one of us who did not realise, in that moment, that we now faced a living replica of those two bodies which had puzzled the medical world. The same massive neck supported the same front-heavy head, from which two intelligent eyes examined us. For clothing he wore nothing but a brown, shapeless tunic and a pair of soft boots.

'As we stared, a voice commanded up to follow, but the dwarf's lips showed no movement. We passed into a large hall lit by some sourceless, diffused radiance. In rows of chairs, we seated ourselves as if for a lecture. The five-foot figure took a chair in front of us.

'It was curious that, in facing the man, I felt none of the distaste one has for an abnormality. It became forgotten that by our standards he was stunted, malformed, hairless, toothless and deaf. He was of another race—no more abnormal than a pygmy or a Tibetan. He addressed us, but still no movement broke his lips.

' "People of the Twenty-Second Century," he formally began, "you are evidently less advanced than we had anticipated. So far, it would appear that you do not accept our offer of transportation, but neither do you reject it—you completely fail to understand it. You must, therefore, be treated like children to some simple demonstrations of our power. First, you shall see the world we offer.'

'Upon the wall behind him, a scene "faded in." Not like a picture, but rather as if we gazed at a real, if fantastic countryside. A level plain stretched away to the distant mountains. In the foreground stood buildings; a city of gleaming metal, each structure beautiful in line and proportion, but none rising higher than two or three floors.

' "The town of Cyp," said the voice. "It stands on the bottom of the old Mediterranean Sea, close by Mount Cyprus. You will notice that it is low-built. This is necessary, as the air at such high altitudes is rarefied. On the Atlantic or Pacific beds"—here the scene changed—"the towns are loftier, since the atmosphere remains dense at such depths. Though the oceans have dried, it is no barren world. The great deeps still contain enough water, and will do so for some hundreds of years. After that is gone, there are the machines."

'A gloomy-looking tarn flashed before us. Deep in its darkness was a reflected glimmer of the red ball of fire above.

' "The Sun is getting old," said the voice. "Slowly he is dying, as he must, but there is a long time yet before his end."

'View began to chase view rapidly across the screen. The voice went on:

' "All this is what we offer in exchange for your world. Buildings which will still be standing proudly when the Earth has become cosmic rubbish as the Moon. Machines to make food, supplement air, create warmth and produce water, all are waiting for you. Machines which are proof against wear, proof against breakdown; wheels which will go on turning when the untenanted world snuffs out the last smouldering fragment of her fiery life.

' "Though much of it will defy your minds, you will have all the accumulation of wisdom and invention that the wit of man has produced since he began. All save one thing—the secret of Time; that is our safeguard, which even we must use with care lest order become chaos."

'Still the scenes flashed and faded before us. Mighty machines, beautiful cities, intricate flowers, limitless plains, vast halls, huge flying cylinders: a panorama of a world shown to us half a million years before it should exist. Most of us were dazed, but we did not doubt. Conviction that this was the truth came not entirely from the voice nor yet entirely from the pictures, but from some power which seemed to accompany both.

'In the presence of the dwarf, the fantastic ceased to be fantastic, and any thought of bluff had long been banished. The case was stated with plain force. He had made us feel that the plan was as feasible as for two nations to change territories —as feasible, and as inconceivable.

'That our population could, if it chose, move half a million years, we had no doubt; but that it would not so choose, we were certain. If the invaders thought that they had but to say the word and we would relinquish our healthy, middle-aged world for one tottering on the brink of senility, they could not know much of our stubbornness.

The tall professor Toone, of Harvard, rose from his seat.

' "On behalf of all of us, I should like to know the reason for this plan," he said. "You appear to offer us much. What do you gain that we lose?"

' "You lose," replied the voice, "nothing but familiar surroundings. We offer better surroundings."

' "But," objected someone, "what about our children? Several generations are safe, you say, but you condemn the rest to extinction?"

' "Some, but not all. You ensure for the others an infinite future—if you understand such a term. That is the object of the plan."

' "But——"

' "Do you not yet realise that we are your descendants—the descendants of your children? We are the race your stock has bred and, though we have climbed far, the end is too near for us. Were we to stay in our age we should die when the Earth died.

' "Instead we shall take the more youthful Earth, for our need is the greater. From it we shall climb to infinity, as life climbed from the sea to the land. Thus will we, your children, approach the closer to our destiny. It was not meant that life should cease with the Earth—evolution was delayed. Do you understand?"

' "Hanged if I do," murmured the man next to me. "What's he getting at? Is it religion?"

'I did not answer him. I was trying to understand. The speech had been far longer than the repetition I have given you. Much of it I still cannot grasp. The vista was too big, the muddle of time too involved, but I thought I had the main drift. The next speaker almost voiced one of the questions which troubled me, though his manner was facetious. He was an Englishman, whose voice sounded tired as he asked:

' "Am I to understand that, though we are at present your ancestors, you are shortly likely to become your own ancestors?"

' "Yes," said the voice, "and no." The Englishman looked helplessly around.

' "I give it up," he announced, in tones even more tired than before.

' "You cannot understand that until you know the nature of time," was the reply. "While you continue to imagine time in terms of progression, you put more stumbling blocks before you than did ever the flat-Earth theorists."

'Professor Toone arose again to put a question. I cannot remember what it was, for at that point the discussion started to leave me behind. Voices went on wriggling into an abstruseness beyond my mental grasp. It was a kind of knock-out contest—the survival of the mentally fittest. When Sir Henry Deen rose to his feet, a long time later, there can only have been two or three of the company who retained any pretensions to following the slender thread of explanation. He broke the spell.

' "Can we be shown something of your works, something concrete upon which we can report? So far, we have done nothing which will profit either you or those who sent us. The public we represent will scarcely be impressed by hearing merely of a philosophical discussion which most of us have failed to follow. Any intimation we could give them of the forms of armament upon which you rely to carry out this plan would be vastly more impressive than an unlimited amount of discussion."

' "You shall look around our building, though there is little to see. In the matter of armament, we must disappoint you," the voice replied. Sir Henry grunted.

' "Intending to keep that secret, eh? Very sensible too, from your point of view; but if you could give a demonstration of your weapons' power . . ."

' "You mistake us," the voice reproved. "We cannot show armament because we have none."

' "Ha! Then the whole thing is a piece of humbug—a bluff. I had suspected so from the beginning. You think that by tricks——"

' "Again you do not understand. Why should we have any need of those guns and shells which are, after all, merely the extension of the Stone Age man's sling and throwing flint? Intellect has no use for such uncertain toys—shells which may kill one man or one hundred men. We wish to kill no one."

'Sir Henry snorted again to show his contempt for such an attitude, or perhaps to be on the safe side in the event of this proving itself an extension of the bluff.

'There was a pause, during which seveal more dwarfs entered and approached our instructor in a manner which revealed them as inferiors. It was explained that we should be shown round the buildings in parties.

' "It's a queer thing," said my neighbour as we rose, "but did you notice that the old boy never opened his mouth all the while he talked to us? Nor has this one." He nodded towards the back of our guide. "Also, we know they can't hear, yet they understand everything we say. Rum, I call it. Just you watch this fellow, now."

'The dwarf strode straight at the metal wall, and a space appeared before him.

' "Nothing queer about that," I said. "I know plenty of doors at home which open when you tread on the mat."

' "No, it's not that. You watch next time. That bit of wall neither swung back nor slid—it just disappeared. Same thing happened when we first came in."

'The guide was frankly contemptuous. His was the manner of a major-domo taking the lap-dog for a walk. He threw out occasional curt references to the objects we passed. These machines were water-producers; those, food-makers. One and all were equally mysterious to most of us. We trailed blankly along, gaping as vacantly as any savage at his first radio.

'Perhaps the dwarf was justified in his contempt, for these machines, unlike the "travellers," did not use Lestrange batteries, and the source of power was to us as obscure as the methods of operation were unintelligible. At length we reached a large hall which, at first glance, seemed to be a jumble of bird-cages.

' "Travelling machines," came abruptly from the guide. We approached them, and he became so informative over what we guessed to be a recent invention that contempt was momentarily forgotten. One of the two rows of dials, he explained, determined the amount of time to be travelled. It contained seven indicators, ranging from an hour to ten thousand years. The lower row regulated the position.

'A certain amount of interaction between the two rows was necessary. For one thing, it prevented the machine from maintaining its position in space without reference to the motion of the Earth. Within the limits set by this interaction, position could be calculated almost to a foot.

' "What's that for?" asked one of the party, reaching towards a lever. As he lifted his hand the dwarf saw him, and he reeled back, crashing to the floor. Afterwards, he told us that it had felt like a tremendous blow between the eyes.

' "What did I tell you?" said my neighbour excitedly. "Force of mind, that's what those people use; that's why their hands are vestigial. Pure will-power."

'The dwarf seemed to hear him, for he looked towards us.

' "I am surprised," he sneered, "that you even know of such a thing as will-power. I judged by your reflexes that you had only instincts."

' "You are insulting," said a voice behind me.

' "There are thirty of you," he continued to sneer. "Let us see if your combined wills assist you against mine."

'We stared around us in amazement. The walls had gone; the machines, too—everything. There was nothing to be seen in any direction save unbroken desert.

' "Playin' Aladdin's lamp tricks," growled my neighbour, bending down to grasp a handful of sand. The dwarf almost smiled at our confusion.

' "You know perfectly well where you are," he said. "But all you can see or feel is the open desert. That's how much all your wills are worth against mine. Try, now, to see whether you can bring the walls round you again."

'I suspect that it was the mind of that remarkable man, Professor Toone, which tipped the scales in our favour. For a moment, we felt the heat still beating up from the sand, then the shadowy outlines of the hall began to re-form. Slowly, from mistiness they grew more substantial; for a few seconds they began to fade again; then, in a flash, we were back indoors. The dwarf lay on the floor before us, panting.

' "Lord!" said someone. "Played out like he'd run ten miles. Anyway, we've got some wills between us!"

CHAPTER FOUR

THE LAST WARNING

'WHEN I had been home three days, I began to understand Professor Toone's decision that the Committee should meet and discuss in Paris before scattering to report. He had made the suggestion during the flight back to Le Bourget. The alacrity of acceptance was such as to make one suspect that the delegates were so uncertain of what their reports should contain that they were eager for a few pointers.

Toone, by common consent, opened the proceedings.

' "Gentlemen," he began, "each of us will be called upon in a few days to give his comments upon the results of our investigation. The questions we shall be asked will appear ridiculous, in the light of our experience, but they will not seem so ridiculous to us as will our answers to our governments. They will say: 'What form of power supported and propelled the flyer you travelled in?' We shall reply that we have no idea. They will be irritated.

' "They will ask: 'How many of these dwarfs are there?' We shall have to reply that we saw, at most, about fifty. They will smile. This will be followed up with: 'What kind of armaments?' We saw none, and have reason to believe that they possess none. 'How many flyers?' We saw only one. 'What is their silvery metal?' We do not know.

' "So it will go on until, with their amusement and their contempt, we shall be in danger of becoming a laughing-stock. If that is allowed to occur, we have no hope of any warning we may give being regarded as anything but further embroidery to a great joke. Seldom, gentlemen, can any committee of investigation have produced less concrete results. Had we found great guns, strange rays, new gases, they would have listened to us. Instead, we have found a menace of pure force, beside which such weapons would be childish.

' "We have found this, I say; but because we cannot comprehend it, we cannot describe it. The grand total of our observation is one strange ship, one equally strange building, a few dwarfs, a number of machines reputed to be time-travellers, other unknown machinery and what our critics will call a cinematograph show. That is all we saw: we cannot tell them what we felt. . . .

' "This, then, is the problem confronting us: How can we convey to a sceptical world the sensation we received of potential force? The peoples must know of that seething mental battery, that surging power of will beside which we are scarcely reasoning creatures—they must know, and they must believe. The burden of their conviction lies upon us.'

'The conference had continued for two days. Two wasted days, they seemed to me. Speeches drifted more and more from the main issue, and gradually tended to confine themselves to suggestions for combating the menace. Again and again Professor Toone dragged the members back from their talk of tactics by his insistence that the governments must first be convinced of the need for tactics. No solution could be suggested short of the governments themselves experiencing our sensations.

'Back home, I was sitting in a palatial office trying to convince a bored official who felt that his time was being wasted. I was growing irritated.

' "Can't you think," I demanded, "in any terms but guns and gases?"

' "They might have ignition rays," he assented. I groaned.

' "Of course they might have, but can't you see what I'm getting at? They simply haven't been developing along those physical lines."

' "They seem to have developed physically a great deal, if your description is accurate."

' "Their present form was probably reached tens of thousands of years ago—to them, that is. It's their minds which have progressed since then. If only you could meet them, you'd begin to feel that terrifying force. Man alive! It was as much as thirty of us, most of them brilliant men, could do to overthrow the mental suggestion of one of their inferior servants."

'The official smiled.

' "And their flyer. . . . Do you realise that there was no one save the Committee on board—no pilot, no crew? The whole blasted thing was worked by a telepathic control of some kind."

' "We also have radio control," he reminded me gently.

'I began to admit to myself what I had known from the first—that it was hopeless. But still I hammered on.

' "You don't realise what they are working for. We speculate mildly about the future of mind—they know its future. They are out for discarnate intelligence. They know that, given time, they can achieve it."

' "Nonsense! There can't be a mind without a brain."

' "Why not? The brain is only the organ of the mind, a sort

of central control for the other organs. Already they can project their minds, but they still have to use the body as a base
for operations."

' "You seriously expect me to believe that?"

' "There's proof of it. Did you hear the voice which issued
their ultimatum?"

' "Yes."

' "And it came from the loud-speaker?"

' "Yes."

' "Then perhaps it will surprise you to know that in London
they took a record of one of the messages. When they put it on
the machine, not a sound was to be heard—the thing was
blank. Those messages never came out of the loud-speaker;
but the dwarfs, for some reason of their own, made you think
—made us all think they did."

'In the evening, when I met Mary, I was tired and discouraged. Nothing I had been able to say had even dented that
wall of mechanical materialism. My most trenchant arguments
had either bounced off or missed fire. The final blow had been
when, in the middle of my efforts to convey my impressions of
mental strength, he had asked, with the air of one who draws
the conversation back to realities, whether I thought they
might have tanks hidden in the neighbourhood.

' "It isn't," I said to Mary, "for or against acceptance of the
dwarfs' terms—as for that, I only know that I, personally, am
going to no dying world. My job was to try to make the fools
realise they really were terms. For over two hours I tried to tell
that smug know-all that an overwhelming danger threatens
him, the nation and the whole world. But I made just as much
impression as I would throwing snowballs at a pyramid."

'Mary gazed at me intently. "It's very difficult to grasp," she
said. "Even yet I don't really understand what this great
danger is, if they haven't got any weapons."

' "That's the devil of it. They may even have some weapons
in the way you mean—though I don't think so—but that is
nothing to do with their strength. Oh, if I could only convey
that sensation which scared us all, something might be possible, but I'm utterly incompetent. If you asked a horse to explain the activities of men, he'd be no more helpless than I am
over this business."

' "But, dear, if there are so few of them, why should they
want the whole world? Surely they could make a sort of colony
somewhere?"

' "I don't know, but I think this is a sort of advance guard—
supervisors of emigration and immigration; we don't even

know how many of them there are. Probably the world couldn't support both populations at once, so that the only way is a complete change-over. Half the worry about this affair is that we know nothing of the details—we're just expected to do as we're told."

'Mary bent towards me, and tried to smooth out the furrows of anxiety.

' "Darling," she said firmly, "you must stop worrying about it. Put it all away for the present."

'She took my arm, and we strolled out on to the terrace. A soft breeze pressed the trees so that they swayed gently. Slips of torn cloud were gliding across the Moon. Far, far away, we could see the misty outline of the hills.

' "It's all so beautiful," she whispered, her eyes on the dim distance. "I think it makes me afraid." My arm went round her.

' "Our lovely world," said my voice.

' "But how long ours?" asked my mind.

'A month later, we were given a glimpse of hell. We were shown our civilisation for what it was worth; how all our vaunted progress had taken us no farther than the first rung of the ladder; and with that rung broken, we were back where we had started.

'For a day and a night, a whole twenty-four hours, the dwarfs stole our power, took away the essential prop of our lives. By what means they made the Lestrange batteries go dead, I can't guess, but they did; and with that our world stopped. Save in the great tide-stations, which still made power for the useless batteries, not a wheel could turn.

'It was chaos. . . . Planes fluttered from the skies, ships wallowed in the seas, airships floated away on the winds, factories were silent, elevators dropped, trains were checked, ovens cooled, radios died, cars were pulled up and every light failed.

'It was nine o'clock at night when the great stoppage came, and it was the darkness which caused the panic. Across the world, in the sunlight, they cannot have had that catastrophic madness in which crowds rushed, milled and swirled without reason, without object. How it was done, nobody knew. Perhaps it was a ray against which they shielded their travellers. Perhaps . . . but what is the use of speculating on the possibilities of such minds?

'I was in the city; the roar of the city's life rose through my open windows. One moment, busy hubbub and bright lights; the next, silence and darkness. I stumbled across the room and

looked out into a pitchy gulf which might have led to the
bowels of the Earth, it was so quiet. It was a quiet which
seemed to wait—a quiet during which men died; during which
cages dropped down mines, divers got no more air, loads fell
from cranes, acrobats missed trapezes, surgeons cut too deep.

'From below there came a scream and, as if at that signal, a
murmuring rose : the voice of the crowd growing louder and
louder, wilder and wilder. My eyes could see nothing, but my
mind saw devilish things happening in that streeet. Bodies
crushing at the walls, ribs cracking under pressure, eyes burst-
ing from their sockets, lungs labouring for air, corpses trampled
underfoot and corpses unable to fall; while above it all rose
now the senseless roar of that wild beast, the mob, destroying
itself.

'I moved back and sought the telephone, only to find it as
dead as the lights. It was not until then that the full meaning
of the crisis came to me. At first it had seemed only an unusual
failure of current. Now I realised, in a flash, just what it
meant, and knew it for the dwarfs' master stroke.

'They had been roused from their patience at last. Of the
several messages sent out on their world-wide system since our
useless investigation, I had heard only one. It was almost
pleading in tone.

' "Our destinies must be worked out; nothing shall stop that.
We wish you no harm—we are not butchers—but you are leaving us no alternative."

'The voice went on to appoint "stations" for transportation.
In the northern plains of Italy; North and South France; near
Johannesburg, South Africa; Salisbury Plain in England; in
Florida, California and Illinois for the United States; and so
on, to the number of sixty or more.

' "I wonder," said one of my companions, "why they always
make these announcements in English?" Another listener, a
blond young man, looked at us.

' "You will excuse?" he said. "But I haf chust heard them
perfect German use, nod English."

'I attempted to explain that the messages were conveyed
directly to their minds without the use of sound; that they
merely thought they heard. After this, each obviously considered me more of a fool than he thought the other.

CHAPTER FIVE

THE EVACUATION OF EARTH

'On the set days, crowds flocked to the starting-places. Except for a few cranks such as daily expect the end of the world, none save the cameramen went from any motive than idle curiosity. A holiday spirit was abroad. There was the prospect of a free show of some sort, and the likelihood of a good laugh at the dwarfs' expense. The cameramen were the only survivors.

'All the world saw the films of what occurred. It was announced that the cinematographers had been allowed to return in order that we might see the simplicity with which transportation was effected, and thereby lose any nervousness restraining us. The particular version I witnessed was taken at one of the American stations and was, I was told, typical of all.

'Around a structure resembling an enormously enlarged "time-traveller" stood a cordon of police and guards. The space enclosed was about two hundred yards square. Reliable witnesses stated that a couple of hours earlier there had been no sign of the glittering framework, with the result that among the majority—still incredulous of the idea of time-travelling—there was a tendency to regard it as a magical piece of construction work, rather than accept the fact that it had just made the journey across five hundred thousand years.

'Beyond the cordon, the sightseers parked their cars and got out to examine the machine with awe. Whatever they had expected in their inmost minds, it was not this huge silver cage; they were impressed in spite of themselves. The murmur of the crowd, as we heard it through the speakers, seemed to betray a nervous tension, but curiosity, backed by a sensation of safety in their numbers, kept them waiting for the show to begin.

'Without warning, parts of the enclosure on all four sides fell apart, making entrances. A gasp of surprise went up from the house as we saw that the guards, whose duty it was to keep the public clear, had stood aside from the gaps. Some of them even motioned the crowd forward.

'Not a sound now came from the speakers. As though in a dream, the sightseers trailed slowly into the enclosure. Suggestion? Hypnotism? Heaven knows. But in they flocked, solemn-faced, vacant-eyed; old men, young men, women and girls alike—even the dogs joined the procession. It was as though some pied piper led the way. Then, when the last had entered, the police and the guards followed.

'In the darkness of the theatre, Mary gripped my arm.

'"Now I begin to understand what you mean by their *power*," she whispered.

'As the last guard entered, the entrances snapped shut. Simultaneously, a few yards from the great "transporter," a dwarf appeared on a one-man "traveller." Mary grew tense, and another gasp rustled through the audience—it was the first time any of them had looked upon one of those men of the far future. He jumped from his machine and ran towards the enclosed crowd, whose apathetic eyes appeared not to notice him.

'In a corner of the transporter, we saw for the first time that a small cabin was divided off from the main bulk. We saw him enter it; we saw him turn the dials, saw his hand upon the lever and—nothing. Nothing before us but the empty plain and a little one-man traveller.

'The picture continued: there was more to come. For five minutes the audience sat in silence or whispered speculation. Then, as suddenly as it had gone, the machine was back again. But, save for the dwarf in his cabin, it was empty. . . .

'The world was roused at last. No type was big enough for the newspapers, no terms weighty enough for the radio announcers. The casualties—as they were determined to call them—at the sixty-odd stations came well on towards the 200,000 mark. The old cry went up—something ought to be done. The prestige of governments was at stake. The vermin must be wiped out!

'The members of the Investigation Committee were hastily summoned, and this time received a better, though no more profitable, hearing. A stern-faced official faced me across a broad desk. His manner suspected me of complicity; his method savoured of third degree.

'"What we want to know first is, where's this base of theirs?"

'"I've told you as near as I can. All I know is that we seemed to go south-south-east from the Algerian coast, as far as I could tell by the Sun. We went that way for about three hours, so if you know the speed of the ship, it ought to give you a rough idea of the district."

'"You must've seen some landmarks, at the height you were."

'"Precious lot of landmarks in that desert—and as we didn't

know beforehand where we were likely to be going, nobody happened to have a pocket-map of the Sahara on him."

' "No need to get fresh. We've got to get a line on this business, somehow, and it'll be better for you if you help us all you can."

' "Well," I said, "I'll tell you this. If you ever find that base, you'll have to thank luck, not cross-questioning."

' "What're you getting at?"

' "Just this. Not one of us has any idea where this place is, or what makes it different from any other place that has a lot of sand; but even if you get there, it's pretty good odds against you seeing the building. Do you seriously think that a gang who can hypnotise a crowd of three or four thousand people into an overgrown bird-cage can't stop a few pilots from seeing them?"

'The man snorted. "When one of our pilots knows where they are——" he began.

' "—then there'll be one less pilot in the force," I finished for him.

'Of course, they got none of the information they wanted from us—we hadn't it. Even then, I had begun to realise that if we knew a whole lot we'd still be as helpless as sheep against men.

'Italian, French, English and German planes scoured the desert, failed to find a trace of the dwarfs' lair and brought home their bombs. A report of the position of the base reached Tripoli. Through hurry, the Italian officers in charge omitted to verify the information. Their rocket-shells destroyed a French desert fort. Feeling already ran high against France, who was thought in some circles to be in league with the dwarfs. Undoubtedly, they were on French territory.

'A French pilot made matters no better by announcing his destruction of the dwarfs' cylindrical flyer at approximately the same moment that the Germans reported that one of their airships had been bombed by a French plane. Notes began to pass between countries, and the threat of war added fuel to the excitement. It was then that someone at the Suez English base made an inventory, with the startling results that five days of profitless searching showed twelve English airships and nearly a hundred planes unaccounted for.

'The French, German, Italian and Egyptian authorities investigated, and revealed a similar state of affairs in their own air forces. The fate of all those craft remained a mystery. Solo searching over the desert became less popular, with the result that, instead of single machines disappearing, whole flights vanished together.

'It fell to an Italian pilot to do the world the worst possible service with the best possible intentions.

'He had become separated from his unit and was heading for home, in accordance with the regulations that single planes must not be risked, when he saw almost below him the shining building for which all the world was searching. Whether his mind was not susceptible to their control, as was found to be the case with a few, or whether they were off their guard, never was known and did not really matter. What did matter was that his five great bombs flashed down together.

'It must have been a rude shock to that pilot when, during his congratulations and celebrations, the voice spoke again.

' "People of the Twenty-Second Century," it began, with usual formality, "we appealed to you first as reasoning creatures. You failed to reason. You even failed to understand. that, if we are not successful, man will count for nothing—will have lived in vain. Then we treated you as children who must be led, and you spoke of it as a tragedy. You described as "casualties" men and women who are now living in the future, not one cell's life the worse for the journey.

' "Now you have taught us to know you for savages. Your ridiculous bombs did no harm to our building, but you killed thirty of our people who were outside. Those thirty were worth a thousand of you, and you killed them by an action no more reasoned than that of a frightened brute. We shall not kill you in revenge—the art of living is not killing—but we warn you that those who remain here three weeks from now will start to kill one another. For the rest, the transporters will be at their stations. Make good use of them."

'Hundreds of thousands laughed. "We've killed some of 'em—we'll beat the lot," was their attitude. But other thousands heeded the warning, surging in crowds to the machines.

'Mary and I were of neither party. I suppose it was sentiment which held us. The road to safety was plain, for the dwarfs never lied, yet the call of familiar things was too strong. We were standing by the world we loved till the last, going down with our civilisation.

'All governments published futile edicts forbidding approach to the transporters. Planes were headed off, trains stopped, roads blocked, but still the crowds swept forward on foot. Infantry and tanks, sent to turn the stream, only joined it. The authorities reached their wits' end.

'The English sent rocket-shells against the Salisbury Plain station. Hundreds of their own people died. The transporter was scarcely scratched. In California, two men, finding themselves immune from the dwarfs' influence, attempted to steal a small time-traveller—and were never seen again. Thereafter, the dwarfs arrived in pairs, one to work the transporter while the other guarded their travellers.

'For the full three weeks, the huge machines made their two or three journeys a day, but the hundreds of thousands they carried were like a few spoonfuls from a full bucket.

'And now, standing in my dark room, I knew that the end had come. Men and women had started to fight insanely, in a frenzy of fear. Soon they would become hungry. They would prowl like famished beasts, ready to eat even each other. It would not be long now, before the multitudes were besieging the only means of escape from a maddened world—the transporters.

'In my mind a plan was growing; a slender chance. First I must get out of this crazy city and find Mary. . . .

'Together we lay in a clump of low bushes. Not far from our hiding-place, a line of haggard men and women was struggling towards a transporter.

' "The evacuation of a world," I heard Mary murmur.

'Some dragged barrows of possessions; some could barely drag themselves. There was no need, now, for suggestion to impel the crowds. They were striving their utmost towards those feared or despised machines, which had become glittering symbols of rescue. Many staggered from fatigue, to fall in their tracks.

' "If the dwarfs use suggestion to help on the fallen ones, count," I said. "They won't need much power, and if you keep your mind full it can't touch you. Fill it up with figures. Multiply and multiply, so that there's room for nothing else. It's our only safeguard."

'Luckily, there was no test of our concentration. Friends pulled the stragglers up and urged them along the last lap of the journey. At last, the transporter was filled; the entrances clicked together. Those who were shut out retired, to throw themselves on the ground. They would have to wait for the next load.

' "Get ready," I whispered to Mary, as I drew a rocket-pistol from my pocket.

'The two small time-travellers appeared. One dwarf ran to the transporter; the other sat on the ground in his saddle. I reckoned that the big machine would be away about twenty minutes, since it would take that long for the weary crowd to file out. As the first dwarf vanished with the transporter, I drew my aim on the second.

'It is a horrible thing to kill a man who is off his guard, but it was necessary. Merely wounded, he might bring his friends about us in a few seconds.

' "Now!" I cried. And together we sprang for the travellers, as the dead dwarf rolled from his seat. "Get on," I ordered, setting the dials. I put Mary's hand on the level. "Pull!" I said. But, instead, she leaned out and pressed her lips to mine.

' "I love you," she said. She said it as though she knew the end had come. Then her hand flew back to the lever. I shouted to stop her, but it was too late—she had gone.'

Jon paused in his tale. We did not interrupt; the grief in his face held us silent.

'Where is she now, I wonder?' he said slowly.

'When she drew back her hands, it brushed one of the dials. I had been so careful, had worked out the position of each to a hair, so that there might be no delay in our coming here; so that we might travel together far away from our world of chaos, far away, too, from the threat of a dying world. One hasty move she made, which may have carried her farther than the Earth's death or beyond its birth. She is a castaway somewhere in the jumble of Time and Space. . . .'

'But you?' asked Lestrange. 'How——?'

'Oh, I jumped on the other machine. The crowd had seen us. A hundred or more of them were pelting across the field. It was as though I had the one lifebelt on a sinking ship. They jumped at me. The traveller rocked as they hit it. It was falling as I pulled the lever—it fell in your laboratory.

'But what's the good of it all? I'm alone. Better to have gone on to the end with the people of my time. Why did I come here when I knew she couldn't be here? If I'd kept the machine, I might have searched—I'd have searched all Time to find her.'

A bell on the wall shrilled suddenly.

'Quick, Wright!' said Lestrange, jumping from his chair. 'The laboratory alarm. Somebody's spying—take this.'

He handed me a pistol, and held one himself. Silently we raced to the laboratory wing, and flung back the door. A familiar silver framework glittered at us. Beside it stood a figure, clad like our visitor.

'Mary, by heaven!' said Jon's voice behind us.

'Jon! Jon!' the figure cried, and ran towards us.

A few moments later, Jon Lestrange walked over to the traveller and examined its controls curiously. He looked up with a smile.

'Obviously, Mary,' he said, 'some patron saint guides your hand. You might have altered the setting by six hundred years, or six thousand, but you did only alter it by six hours.'

He turned towards Professor Lestrange.

'If you please, great-great-great-grandfather,' he said, 'I should like another piece of string.'

INVISIBLE MONSTER

CHAPTER ONE

THE 'HURAKAN' RETURNS

'LISTEN!' said Dirk.

'Look!' said David.

'Hell's bells!' said Toby, and stopped the car.

'All out, quick! It's coming,' Dirk warned them. He opened the rear door and tumbled out, with a cascade of bait tins, baskets, rods and reels. By the time he had disentangled himself, the others were already jumping into the ditch. He joined them.

The sky was full of a rumbling and roaring. From the west, a huge plane bore dead towards them as if intent on their destruction. With the rising Sun on her, she gleamed like molten silver; the plume of fire from her rear rockets stretched out like the tail of a minor comet, and she thundered like all the artillery in the world. A noise to stun, and a sight to terrify.

She grew still larger as she came. She seemed bound to strike the ground where they crouched, but she did not. Instead she passed perhaps a hundred feet above the hill-crest where they cowered with their fingers in their ears. Great, roaring waves of sound buffeted them like physical blows. A wind wrenched as if it would tear their clothes from them. The standing car lurched in its force, and all but overturned. A surge of spent flame seemed to shrivel them, and they gasped in the sulphurous air. But for all that, their heads turned to follow the plane as she sped on.

Toby's lips were moving. His words were inaudible, but his expression said all that was necessary. Rapidly, the plane sank lower. She seemed to touch the tree-tops across the valley. A moment later, she hit. There was a spurt of pure white flame; she leapt twisting into the air, and then disappeared. The sound came rolling back to them, a mighty detonation capping the roar of the rockets. Then silence....

The three men took their hands from their ears and looked dazedly at one another.

'God, what a crash!' shouted David, above his deafness. Dirk climbed back on to the road.

'What the devil was it, anyway?' he demanded. 'It wasn't like any of the big strato-planes I've ever seen. Short, dumpy wings that didn't look as if they could lift her at all; and her lines were all funny, somehow.' He looked inquiringly at the others. David shook his head.

'Got me beat,' he confessed. 'Must have been experimental—on trial, I'd say.'

Toby climbed back into the driving-seat, and started up.

'Shove that junk back and pile in, Dirk,' he directed. 'The fishing expedition's off. I'll be mighty surprised if anyone could have lived through a crash like that, but we're going to see.'

It was eight o'clock before they reached the wreck. Tracks were scarce, and it was impossible to bring the car closer than a mile. For the rest, they had to walk through the woods.

The big plane had come to her final rest in a clearing. Behind her lay a furrow of scattered and scorched trees which she had ploughed away. Her stern portion was tilted up, so that the rocket-tubes pointed at the sky. Her bows were a shapeless, tangled mass, while her middle showed several gaping splits. Even in her crumpled condition, her lines remained puzzling. David, looking at her with the memory of the crash fresh in his mind, was surprised that she had retained even a semblance of her former shape.

The three of them stepped from the trees and crossed the open space together, Dirk asking again:

'But what is she? I swear there's nothing like her on any of the regular statosphere services.'

She was no less puzzling as they drew near. David led the way to the bows, looking for her name. They stopped, surveying the wreckage. The massive steelium plates had crumpled like paper, and all the six port-holes were smashed and gaping. Jagged ends of twisted framework protruded here and there like picked bones. The identification number was buried somewhere beneath the pile of inter-locked rubbish.

David was about to turn back towards the stern when Toby gave an exclamation. At his feet lay a broken section of steelium plate still bearing faintly the outlines of three letters.

'K—A—N,' he read out. 'What country's that?'

David frowned for a moment, and looked puzzled. Then an incredulous expression came over his face. He looked at the wreck again, wide-eyed.

'My God! The *Hurakan*,' he said. The others stared.

'I believe you're right,' said Dirk, at last. 'Yes, it is the *Hurakan*.'

The three of them gazed, awestruck. It was no strato-plane, but a space-ship—Earth's fourth space-ship. One had gone to the Moon, and returned. Two had set out for Mars, and never been heard of since. The fourth, the *Hurakan*, had shot out, a year ago, bound for Venus. And now she was home—what was left of her.

'What an ending! Poor devils,' said David, at length. 'Just on the last lap. I wonder why they crashed? They can't be— still, we'd better look,' he added, and led the way to one of the gaping cracks in the hull.

The other two, after a momentary hesitation, followed him within. They found themselves in a well-built sleeping cabin, which had been unoccupied at the time of the crash. David was thankful for that. He was not hankering for unpleasant sights. Toby strode across to the door in the opposite wall, and tugged at the handle. As he expected, it was jammed, and considerable leverage was necessary to free it. When at last, beneath their united efforts it did give way, the three men were precipitated into a main corridor.

Toby had had the forethought to come equipped with an electric torch. He drew it, now, and flashed the beam around. To the left, leading forward, a tangle of twisted metal choked the way, but to the right the floor stretched away bare and empty, jerked from the straight where the sections of the ship had strained apart. They had taken only a few steps when a splintering crash, somewhere towards the stern, made them stop short. David jumped at its unexpectedness.

'What was that?' he asked uneasily.

'Cooling off, probably,' Dirk guessed. 'She would be in a fine state of heat by the time she hit. Some bits of the wreck-age must still be contracting.'

Nevertheless, there was a discouraging eeriness about these sounds aboard a dead ship, which none of them relished. Per-haps, David thought, they had been mistaken, and someone had managed to survive the impact. He raised his voice in a hail. The echoes sped depressingly about the metal walls, but there was no reply.

Toby led on. Thirty feet along the corridor, a door to the left stood slightly ajar. They pushed it back, and found them-selves in a small living-room, dimly lighted by an empty port-hole. The furnishing was simple, consisting of a desk, a table, three or four chairs and a bookshelf with bars to hold the books in place. But the discovery which most interested David was that the walls were lined with charts, which he and Dick stopped for a moment to examine. They held little interest for Toby, however; and with a word to the other two, he left them to continue his exploration of the ship.

David, poring over a chart on which was a thick, red line, was about to remark upon it to Dirk, but a sudden sound stopped him in mid-sentence. The same cracking, crushing noise which had startled them before, became audible again. This time it was far louder, and seemed closer. Then, hard upon it, came Toby's voice calling them. They stared at each other.

The cry was repeated with a note of alarm, and with one accord they made for the door. A few yards away, the ship's broken back had caused the floor to tilt upwards; and as they scrambled up the slippery metal, they called back encouragingly. The quality of the second cry was hard to associate with Toby: it gave a sense of rising panic. A rattle of pistol shots ahead spurred them on still further. What was there to fire at? Dick wondered.

'Where are you?' he called. Toby's voice answered from the right, and simultaneously there came another wrenching creak of metal. David thrust back a door, and the two of them stood gazing within.

They faced a square store-room. The walls were lined with deep shelves and rows of lockers, save for a space in the middle of the right-hand wall, where both shelves and the partition behind them had fallen away to reveal a dark aperture. The light from the two small port-holes was uncertain, but it seemed to David that the edges of the dark gap bulged and bent even as he looked at them. Away in the left-hand corner crouched Toby, his eyes fastened on the dark hole.

'What———?' David began stepping into the room.

'Stop!' Toby switched his gun on him. 'Don't come a step nearer—there's something nasty loose about here.' The pair noticed that their arrival had taken the note of panic from his voice, but for all that, his manner was tense.

'But———'

'For God's sake, do what I tell you! Now stand back and hold that door open—and clear right out of the way. I've got to jump.'

David obeyed, wonderingly. There seemed no sane reason why Toby should want to jump. Puzzled, he watched the other kick off his shoes and throw down his jacket. He tossed his pistol across, and crouched tensely. Both of his friends knew him to be the possessor of no mean muscles, but the power of his standing jump amazed even them. Toby launched himself in a magnificent leap which would have done credit to an acrobat. It was superb; but it was not enough.

In mid-air, he was suddenly checked. The others gave an astonished cry. Toby had struck something—an invisible something which stood between them. For a second, he seemed to hang in the emptiness, scrambling madly with legs and arms; then he began to slip, first slowly, and then more rapidly, for all the world as if he slid down a curved surface to the floor.

David and Dirk stared in stupefaction as the other struggled and fought, with wildly threshing limbs, against something unseen. David broke the spell, and took a step forward, but Toby noticed the move.

'No, no! Go away!' he shouted. 'I'm done. I——'

His voice broke into a scream of agony, and his body slumped inertly. Half-way up one thigh, a deep line appeared; then, as though severed by an axe, the leg came away with a jerk. But it did not fall; instead it started to drift slowly across the room. With incredulous horror, they saw that the limb was unsupported. It travelled some nine inches above the ground, creeping with a steady, unswerving motion towards the break in the wall. Foot first, it edged inch by inch out of the room, into the darkness beyond.

David's senses were reeling. He felt Dirk's grip on his arm, and tried to speak, but his mouth was queerly dry. He forced his eyes back to the fallen Toby, and caught a sudden breath. An arm, like the leg, was being detached: there was the same sharp indentation, but still no visible agent. As the arm jerked free, he saw that the denuded shoulder was scored by deep grooves.

He sprang back, pulling Dirk with him. Both knew that Toby was past all help, and in a wordless panic, they clattered and slid down the sloping corridor to seek safety in the open.

CHAPTER TWO

PREY OF THE UNSEEN

A FIVE-MILE dash in the car brought them to the townlet of Clidoe. In the police station, they poured out a confused statement to a stolid and unsympathetic sergeant. There was reproving suspicion in the glance with which he favoured them.

An excited entrance coupled with rambling incoherence was, in his experience, frequently to be associated with excess of alcohol. Accordingly, he hid his likeable, though not very brilliant, self behind a stern and chastening stare.

'Just who are you, and what are you doing?' he demanded.

David gave their names, and explained. The sergeant approached and scrutinised them more closely. They were excited, but he had to admit that they showed none of the signs of intoxication. Furthermore, the time was barely eleven o'clock.

'Well,' he said, returning to his desk and picking up a pen, 'suppose you tell it to me all over again, but slowly this time.'

Evidently the alcoholic theory was merely shelved, for his tone was not encouraging. David pulled himself together, and with occasional promptings from Dirk, recounted the affair in orderly detail. The sergeant listened throughout with an air of defensive reserve, more than tinged with disbelief. At the end of the recital, he said:

'I've had a report that a ship went over at an excessive speed, some hours ago. What did you call her?'

'The *Hurakan.*' David spelt out the name. 'You know—the one they sent to Venus.'

The sergeant grunted. 'Now, just what was this—er—assailant like?'

'That's just what I've been telling you. It wasn't like anything. You couldn't see it.'

'It was too dark in the ship?'

'No, I tell you, it was invisible.'

'Invisible, eh? And yet it killed a man?' His voice was a trifle weary. 'What's this you're trying—a hoax?' he demanded, with a sudden change of tone.

He watched them keenly while they both protested vehemently. He had no longer any doubt that the men had received a shock, but this yarn was pretty much like spook stuff.... He pulled one ear reflectively and frowned. The matter would have to be cleared up.

'Rankin,' he called over to a constable, 'you've heard these men's story. Get along, now, and check up on it.'

'Yes, sir.' The constable saluted, and turned to go.

'I'll show you the way,' David suggested.

'No, can't allow that,' the sergeant said firmly. There was something queer behind this. At any rate, one man was dead, and he was taking no chances. 'I'll have to ask you to stay here until Constable Rankin makes his report.'

'But you don't realise! This thing, whatever it is, is dangerous, damned dangerous. We could show——'

'No. If it's serious, I'm going to hold you—if it's a joke, you're going to pay.'

The two gazed helplessly at each other. Dirk shrugged his shoulders.

'Oh, all right.' David subsided on a hard bench and gazed moodily at a framed card of police regulations. 'But don't blame me for anything that may happen,' he added. 'I've warned you.'

Constable Rankin strode unemotionally out of the station, and they heard him start up a motor-cycle. The sergeant began to make laborious notes with a scratchy pen.

Three hours later, at almost two o'clock, the sergeant began to look worried. There had been ample time for a ten-mile ride and a cursory examination. He began to feel misgiving, sharpening into definite apprehension. He plied the two men with a fresh batch of questions, and the answers did little to relieve his mind. Neither David nor Dirk had any doubt as to the reason for Constable Rankin's prolonged absence, and they said as much. The thought of the man calmly walking to such a death stirred a queasiness in their stomachs.

'We'll give him another half-hour. If he's not back by then, we'll go and have a look,' the sergeant said, uneasily.

It was after three when they arrived, reinforced by two constables, at the spot where they must leave the car. David led the silent party through the trees. The two reserve policemen strode forward with puzzled stolidity, while the sergeant wore a worried look which showed that his disbelief had weakened. As they came within sight of the fallen ship, he drew a whistling breath.

'Lord, what a ship—and what a crash!' he murmured. His attitude to the others underwent a subtle change as he asked: 'Now, at which break did you enter?'

David pointed to the gap near the bows. 'Through there,' he said; 'and we began working back to the stern. The store-room must have been about amidships.' He felt a little sick at his memory of that room. The sergeant nodded.

'You lead the way, and show us exactly what happened,' he suggested. David and Dirk both shook their heads emphatically.

'I'll be damned if I do,' said the former. 'I've told you how dangerous it is—and then you tell me to go ahead. That's not good enough.'

The sergeant gave a contemptuous snort, and motioned his

men on. They were half-way across the clearing when there came the sound of splintering, yielding metal. The two friends looked at each other and hesitated.

'What's that?' asked the sergeant, sharply. 'Somebody looting her, I'll be bound. We'll catch 'em in the act.'

A few yards from the break, he halted and began to give instructions in an undertone. After one sentence, he was interrupted by a further creaking and wrenching of metal plates; then they all swung about and gazed sternward. Incredulously, they saw that the side of the ship was bulging. One of the plates of solid steelium was slowly bending outward. Fascinated and speechless, they watched this toughest of metals bulge still farther. The sergeant gasped audibly, for he knew the well-nigh fabulous strength of the material.

The rivet heads stripped off with a rattle like a monster machine-gun in action, and the plate fell outside with a crash. The five men continued to stare nervously, but nothing emerged. Whatever had provided the tremendous force behind the plate remained unseen. The sergeant pulled himself together with an effort.

'We'll start there,' he said. 'Keep close to the hull as we work up, and we'll take them by surprise.'

David and Dirk hung back, and did their best to dissuade him, but he was not to be put off. His manner held a curtness which covered no little misgiving. The party edged along beneath the overhanging side of the ship. Eight feet from the recent hole, their fears were justified. The foremost policeman gave a sudden bellow and leaped back.

'What the——?' the sergeant began, but his words dried up and his eyes widened in astonishment. Pain was ousted momentarily by surprise even in the injured man. He stood, with blood streaming from his severed wrist, gaping inanely at his lost hand as it floated slowly away in mid-air.

David snatched a handkerchief from his pocket, and sprang forward to make a tourniquet. The sergeant recovered rapidly from his first shock, hesitated and seemed about to advance.

'Don't be a fool,' said Dirk, gripping his arm. 'It'll get you, too.'

The sergeant retreated a pace, his eyes still fixed on the moving hand. Without audible comment, he watched it drift into the dark opening. As he turned to the others, his face was pale.

'I've got to apologise to you two gentlemen. I didn't realise what you'd seen. And to think I sent poor Rankin——'

He broke off at the sound of creaking metal. The plates to either side of the original hole were bending and sagging ominously. The party beat a hasty retreat, carrying the injured man, now in a dead faint. In silence, they watched the contiguous steelium being torn slowly and relentlessly from its rivets, until there was a hole in the *Hurakan*'s side four times as large as before.

David, at a safe distance, circled round to catch a glimpse of the interior. He was looking, he knew, at approximately the spot where Toby had met his end, but the walls of the storeroom were now reduced to so much warped and mangled metal on the floor. Of the broad, wooden shelves and lockers which had lined it, there was no sign. Vaguely, he wondered what had become of them; they ought to have been lying crushed with the metal. The sergeant came up to him with all dignity cast aside. It was evident that he now felt well out of his depth.

'I'll have to get help. Will you take a message for me to the Police Station? And there's Dawkins, too,' he nodded towards the injured policeman. 'He needs treatment as soon as he can get it. If you and your friend would take him in the car while we keep watch here ...?'

David agreed. He waited while the sergeant scribbled a note; then he and Dirk, bearing the unconscious man between them, moved off towards the car.

At five o'clock, after they had dropped the unfortunate Dawkins at the hospital and reinforced themselves with a good meal, they returned to find that the force of police at the *Hurakan* had been considerably augmented. The sergeant greeted them with undisguised gloom. He pointed out that the hole was much enlarged, and that further plates had been wrenched off in other parts.

'Hanged if I know what to do,' he admitted. 'The inspector ought to be along any time now, thank the Lord. Though I don't know what he'll be able to do about it, either. Just look at this.'

He picked up a stout branch some three inches in section, and holding it extended before him, advanced cautiously towards the gaping hole. A six-inch length was lopped off with a crunch. He retreated hurriedly and came back, pointing to deep, gouged grooves in the wood.

'Teeth,' he said; 'not a doubt.'

David nodded. It reminded him, unpleasantly, of Toby's shoulder. He looked quickly back at the ship, and remarked on the number of fresh breaches in her sides.

'And that's not all.' The sergeant indicated a small bush which grew four or five yards away from the ship. 'Watch that,' he said.

The bush was cracking and bending towards them beneath invisible pressure. It gave way as they looked, and was crushed into a mass. Then it lifted slightly above the ground and began to drift in the wake of the piece of branch, on a slow journey to the ship.

'It's big, and it's advancing,' added the policeman. He picked up a stone and tossed it high into the air. Its curving flight towards the hull was uncannily interrupted. It hung for a moment, before rolling a yard down and sideways. Then it rested, to all appearances unsupported, and stationary save for a slight pulsating rise and fall. All the watching men felt a touch of that trepidation which is bred by the incomprehensible.

A startling shriek from the other side of the ship stung them into action. They rounded the stern, to collide with a group of men and women travelling at a surprising speed.

'What's wrong here?' the sergeant demanded. One of the men pointed behind him and shouted something unintelligible as he ran on.

'Damned sightseers,' puffed the sergeant. 'Just as well they're scared. Can't they run, though?'

With a full view of the other side, they stopped. The reason for the runners' panic became plain. One sightseer would pry no more. His body, in dismembered sections, was drifting towards the ship.

David looked at Dirk, and then turned to the other. He was feeling sick with the sights of the day, and suggested that they might be allowed to leave. The sergeant nodded.

'Yes. It wouldn't do me much good to keep you here now, but I'd like you to be handy tomorrow—the inspector may want to have a word with you both.' He produced a large handkerchief and mopped his face. 'That is,' he added, 'if the inspector ever turns up.'

CHAPTER THREE

THE GROWING MENACE

T H E two succeeded in finding a passable hotel in Clidoe, and returned the next morning to find that the inspector had at last arrived and taken command. Little had been possible during the night beyond the posting of guards to warn off the curious, but with daylight, a phase of activity had set in. A judicious tossing of stones had determined roughly the extent of the danger area, and it had become apparent that it now extended all about the ship in an approximate oval. The actual verge, however, was by no means regular, since here and there, invisible extensions projected three or four feet in advance of the main substance.

Rows of sticks, planted at regular intervals, had enabled the average speed of advance to be estimated at something over a yard an hour. The sergeant, again on the scene, greeted them and expressed his doubts of the value of this calculation.

'It may be,' he pointed out, 'that this is not an advance at all, as they mean it, but merely the normal rate of growth.'

'God forbid!' said David fervently.

'What scientists have they got on the job?' asked Dirk.

'None. They reckoned they could tackle this thing all right without them—it'd mean extra expense to bring them along.'

Dick grunted. 'Probably save you expense in the end,' he commented.

They looked out across the clearing. Save for the increased number of holes in her sides, the *Hurakan* looked just as they had first seen her the previous day. The sunlight bathed her, glittering in sparkling flashes from her polished plates. To all appearances, there was nothing amiss between her and them; nothing to stop one from walking right up to her and entering. Staring intently one could fancy, perhaps, the slightest haze about her; something more tenuous than rising heat, but enough to make the edges not quite sharp. Nevertheless, David realised that, unwarned, he would have walked right into the invisible trap without a suspicion.

With the relinquishing of his responsibility to the inspector, the sergeant's spirits had become more normal. The other had taken over without enthusiasm, and was now a troubled man. He nodded in a depressed way to David and Dirk, as they came up, and asked a few questions in a tone which showed that he expected little help from them. A few minutes later, a man in military uniform strolled across from the protecting cordon, and introduced himself.

He was, it seemed, a Captain Forbes, and not unpleased with the fact. He gazed across at the *Hurakan* in a bored style, and his manner was a blend of faint amusement and superiority. He spoke of his commander who had sent him, but had given no reason.

'Well, Inspector,' he said, 'you've certainly managed to stir up our people—they've sent me along to reinforce you with a party of men and a machine-gun. What's it all about?'

The sergeant explained the situation again; and the inspector, though he had heard it before, listened to his subordinate with an expression of increasing anxiety. At the end of the report, and David's description of Toby's end, he nodded slowly and gazed thoughtfully towards the ship.

'As we have no more evidence to go on, we must conclude that the crash killed all the men aboard and set free some queer specimen they were bringing home with them, as our young friends here seem to think. Or else that the thing got free on the journey, attacked them and possibly killed the only men competent to land the ship properly. But there's no proof which it was.'

Captain Forbes, with a scepticism born of little imagination, protested.

'But that sounds absurd. What do you reckon the thing is?'

David disclaimed all pretence of knowledge, but suggested that it was some kind of animal. It might equally well be a plant, he admitted, but he thought not.

Captain Forbes smiled with a kindly tolerance, lit a cigarette and began to saunter towards the ship. Dirk caught him by the arm.

'Don't be a fool! I don't blame you for not believing us, but take a look at this.'

He caught up the branch which the sergeant had dropped the previous day, and exhibited the teethmarks. The captain examined them with close attention, and lost his ambition to advance at the moment.

The inspector turned to David.

'You've thought of no way of tackling this thing, I suppose?'

David shook his head. Dirk chimed in: 'I've thought of one thing which may, or may not, be important.'

'And that is?'

'To prevent it from reaching the trees, if possible. You notice that it has consumed all the wood it has found. That may be merely a method of removing obstruction, but I doubt it: it didn't deal with the metal that way. I shouldn't be surprised to find that it feeds on wood.'

With his eye, the inspector measured the distance between the wreck and the trees—a quarter was already covered in the majority of places. Captain Forbes fidgeted impatiently.

'Look here, Inspector, I know this is your show, but what about letting me try my machine-gun on the thing—that'll tear it to bits.'

The other hesitated, and then agreed. He had little faith in the power of a machine-gun against the creature—if such it was—but no harm seemed likely to result. As the captain strolled off, a thought struck him, and he scribbled a few words on a piece of paper which he handed to a constable with instructions for him to hurry.

A puzzled-looking party of machine-gunners arrived, and was steered into position a few yards from the danger line. When it was explained that they were to set up their weapon at this spot, they appeared at first resentful, and then amused. They planted the gun with the air of men who humoured the half-witted.

'Bit o' target practice—only there ain't no target,' muttered one of them,

The gunner settled himself. 'What do we aim for, sir?'

'Just aim straight ahead.'

The man shrugged his shoulders nonchalantly, and drummed a short burst. The crew gasped audibly. Each bullet had uncannily mushroomed out, and now hung, a splotch of lead, in mid-air.

'Can't say as I like this,' one of the men muttered nervously. 'What the hell is it, anyway?'

The gun choked out another rattling burst, with identical results. David shot a sidelong glance at the captain; the expression of the latter was highly gratifying. The gunner turned an astonished face.

'Any more, sir?' he inquired.

'Look out!' shouted David. The blobs of lead had risen and surged forward. The gun crew, now thoroughly rattled, jumped back. One man tripped over the tripod and fell. There came a crunching sound, followed by a cry of agony—and the man's boot, with his foot still inside, began to move slowly away. His companions turned and dragged him back.

Captain Forbes's face turned a peculiar colour as he stared foolishly at the severed foot. For the first time, it seemed to dawn on him that the affair was not a hoax, after all.

'Well, your machine-gun hasn't cut much ice,' commented the inspector, unkindly. 'When they bring the stuff I've sent for, we'll try another trick.'

They were forced to wait for half an hour before a small party appeared carrying a bulky object, which a closer view revealed to be a bale of cotton-waste. Behind them followed two more men carrying cans of petrol.

'Soak the stuff,' directed the inspector, as they lowered it. 'Pour the lot over it—and get some long poles.'

The lighted bale flared furiously. Four men approached and began to lever it forward with the poles, while the rest stood intently awaiting the outcome.

'If it's a success, we'll get some flame throwers,' the inspector was saying.

The bale came to an abrupt stop as it met the unseen barrier. It rested there, flaming smokily.

'Push again!'

The obstruction had withdrawn, and the bale was able to advance a full turn before the next check. The sergeant showed what for him was unusual excitement.

'Bit hot for it,' he gloated. 'We've got it moving, now!'

But he was too optimistic. Just as the poles came forward for a further thrust, there came a thud which shook the ground; the flames were snuffed out, and nothing but a charred smear remained of the flattened bale. The pole-holders speedily retreated.

'Damned if it hasn't jumped on it!' snorted the sergeant indignantly.

The inspector pushed back his cap and scratched his head. His expression, as he gazed towards the *Hurakan*, was one of utter loss. Captain Forbes was no less taken aback, but after a few minutes' thought, he broke into a smile. He stepped closer to the inspector, and made a suggestion. The other looked doubtful.

'I'll have to get permission,' he demurred. 'After all, someone owns the ship.'

'They won't mind when they understand the danger. Much better destroy the ship than let this thing grow.'

'How long will you take?'

Captain Forbes considered. 'Till tomorrow morning.'

The inspector nodded. The plan seemed sound. Nevertheless, he glanced uneasily at the line of measuring sticks. The danger area would be close to the trees by the next morning. The captain saw his look and interpreted it rightly.

'I know you'd like to tackle the thing now, but what can we do?'

Dirk, who had watched the last two attacks on the creature without comment, walked over to them. The inspector's attempts to come to grips with the danger seemed to him childish and highly unscientific. He was reminded of some boys he had once seen poking a sleepy lion with sticks—but there was a difference, for the boys had been able to rely upon the protection of the bars. Now, Captain Forbes had succeeded in producing something which was probably another hairbrained scheme.

'Why not get some biologists on the job?' he suggested.

The captain did not receive the remark kindly. There was no reason that he could see why a terrestrial biologist should be an authority on a form of life imported from Venus—if, indeed, it had come from there. Moreover, he pointed out that you did not call in a biologist when you wanted to destroy even an Earthly wild animal. Dirk was curt.

'That's just what you should do. After all, it was the biologists who destroyed the pests in Panama and similar unhealthy spots. For all you know, you may be fooling around with a barrel of high explosives. Just suppose the creature had been inflammable, as it might easily have been—you'd have started a fire which would have spread for miles.'

'You are not a biologist yourself?' asked the captain coldly.

'I am not.'

'Then I'll thank you not to interfere. Further, I will remind you that you have no standing here.'

The inspector, less sure of himself, made to interrupt, but changed his mind. He did not feel a great deal of confidence in the captain, but he sympathised with his resentment. Dirk's face went red with anger.

'While you're playing around, this thing is growing. If it gets right out of hand, Lord knows what may happen—and the responsibility for it will be yours!'

'That being so, will you please refrain from further comment? Since you seem to have no constructive help to offer, I see no reason for you to remain here.'

Dirk checked the retort which occurred to him. He turned on his heel and strode angrily away into the trees.

'Damned meddler,' muttered the captain as he watched him go. Turning back to the inspector, he added: 'If we are to be ready by tomorrow morning, I'll need to get busy immediately.'

CHAPTER FOUR

THE MONSTER MULTIPLIES

DIRK did not return to the hotel, nor did he leave any message. David was scarcely surprised, for Dirk was not one of those to take rebuke easily, the less so when it was scarcely merited. In consequence, he made a solitary breakfast the next morning.

There was no mention of the *Hurakan* affair in any of the newspapers. He had expected headlines in elephantine type, but repeated search failed to reveal even a paragraph on the subject. It was the more perplexing since the ship had now lain on the hillside two nights and two days. On his way to the scene, he stopped at the police station and picked up the sergeant.

'What's happened to the journalists?' he asked as they started. 'This ought to be a godsend to them.'

'It was, but we shut down on them.'

'That's a notable achievement—but why?'

'They were going to spread themselves; there'd have been day trips running by this time and—well, you remember what happened to that sensation-seeker the other day. Besides, there are going to be some fireworks today, and we want the place clear.'

They approached the wreck to find that the danger area had shown a greater increase than had been expected. Only a narrow margin of safety, of a few yards' breadth, now lay between it and the trees. The inspector and Captain Forbes looked up to greet them, and then returned to the study of an enlarged photograph. David gave an exclamation of surprise, and the captain grinned.

'Good, isn't it? Just been delivered.'

'But how on Earth——?'

'Bit of brainy work up at the Flying Field. They sent a plane over yesterday and fired off a few feet of film—naturally, there wasn't a sign of the thing when they developed. Then some bright lad had the idea of rigging up an infra-red camera, and sent it over. Here's the result.'

The print showed the site of the *Hurakan* and the immediate neighbourhood. Of the ship herself, little but the upper surface was visible, the rest being submerged in a dark area which extended all about her. At first glance, this shadow appeared to be a smooth oval, but a closer view revealed that the edge was serrated into a series of blunt projections. David found it disappointing, and said so.

'Can't tell much from that,' he murmured. 'I mean, it still doesn't show us whether we are dealing with a single creature or a mass of the brutes.'

'Anyway, I'm certain that it is animal and not vegetable,' rejoined the inspector. 'And that's not really so strange, when you come to think of it. After all, it's not a very great step from the transparent living things we have on Earth, to a creature of complete invisibility. Did you notice that everything that it has snapped up travelled right into the ship? I have an idea that we shall find it to be one individual with multiple throats, and a central stomach somewhere in the *Hurakan*. In fact, Captain Forbes' plan is really built upon that idea.'

'What is the plan?'

The inspector explained. It had been calculated that any object snatched by the invisible creature would require—at its present size—just over two minutes to travel into the ship. A number of bombs had been constructed, and equipped with timing devices to give a further half minute's grace. They had then been placed in wooden cases, to make them palatable to the creature; and he had every hope that the simultaneous explosion of this indigestible meal would settle the matter. It entailed, of course, the annihilation of the ill-fated *Hurakan*, but she could now be of little value.

'Why not detonate the bombs by short waves and make certain that they coincide?' David asked.

The captain shook his head. 'That was the first idea, but there's the masking effect of the metal hull to be considered, and it's quite likely that the body of the creature may act in some degree as a shield. The timing method seems more certain.'

David stood back and watched the preparations. Forty or fifty men had been assembled, and the captain was instructing them in their duties. The sergeant came to his side and chatted. He seemed to have no great faith in the plan, and concluded with the opinion that they had better look for cover if they did not wish to be blown to pieces themselves. David recalled seeing a disused hut which would be ideal for the purpose, since it stood back in the woods a hundred yards from the main clearing. He led the way around the narrow, free space which still remained.

At a convenient spot, they paused to look at the deployment of the captain's troops. At regular intervals, all around the edge of the clearing, men were taking up positions facing the ship. At a glance, it seemed impossible that there could be any danger lurking in that sunlit space—it still appeared that one might walk right up to the *Hurakan*'s glittering sides and encounter no more obstacle than the empty air. Each of the encircling men held a pole in his right hand, on the end of which was mounted the wood-cased bomb, while in his left hand was a string attached to the pin. One or two of them were noticeably nervous, and others seemed to regard the whole affair in the light of a joke. The majority waited phlegmatically for the signal.

At the sound of three sharp whistle blasts, each pole-bearer snapped into sudden action. The weapons were tilted horizontally, the left hands tugging smartly at the strings, and the pins fell free. The cordon closed with levelled staves, in the manner of old-time pikemen.

They took three paces, and then a sharp crackling ran around the line as the bulbous wooden heads were snapped away, to begin their slow journey to the wreck. The men of the cordon sprinted for cover, dropping their shortened poles as they went. For a full half-minute, David and the sergeant continued to watch the uncanny progress of the flock of destructive balls, slowly and silently converging. Then, they, too, thought of shelter and made for the hut.

The meagre light from two grimy windows enabled David to inspect the place. Such furnishings as had occupied it had long since been removed. Only a few sagging shelves were left; a broken axe-shaft and remnants of other tools lay about, with a few dribbled paint cans and other rubbish not worth the labour of removal. He sat himself down on a pile of leaves in one corner. The sergeant came and joined him. Their heads bent together over a large, business-like watch of the latter's.

'Still a minute to go.'

As if in prompt contradiction came a muffled, double thud, quickly followed by a third. The sergeant shook a disapproving head. Bad workmanship—luckily it didn't matter a great deal in the present circumstances. Increasingly tense, they watched the second hand crawling towards the main burst. It came fifteen seconds before it was due. First a crash, and then, right on top of it, a stunning roar, as though the premature explosion of one bomb had fired the rest.

Instinctively, they clapped their hands over their ears, while great waves of sound sent the windows tumbling into fragments. They were battered and swirled around, as the aerial breakers surged over them. A patter of scattered debris rained overhead, and a violent thud caused the entire structure to tremble. Dislodged dirt rattled down, and closely following it came the slither of something falling from the sloping roof. It landed with a soggy thump outside the door.

David grinned. 'I'll bet that was a part of the brute,' he said with satisfaction. 'If it gets over that little meal, it'll——'

He stopped suddenly. Somewhere near at hand had risen a scream of fear, a scream mounting in agony till it stopped with a suggestive suddenness. The two looked at each other in consternation. That scream could only mean one thing—something had gone wrong, and the danger was not past. The sergeant opened his mouth to speak, but was silenced by another tearing scream, closer than the first.

For some minutes after that, the air rang with anguished cries. David clapped his hands back over his ears to shut out the sounds of torment. He darted a glance at the sergeant, and could see that his face was pale and grimly strained; he was rising in the manner of one who feels that he should act, but does not know what course to take. He stepped towards the door, but David was swifter; he rushed past him and stood barring the way.

'No,' he cried. 'Give me that stick first.'

Wonderingly, the other picked it up and handed it to him. David pulled the door an inch or two ajar, and thrust the stick downward through the slit. There was a swift crunch, and he withdrew it, appreciably shorter.

'You see?' He pointed to the unmistakable marks of teeth at the end of the stick.

The sergeant took it from him; and then he, too, thrust it at the crack—higher up than before. He struck smartly downwards. Two feet from the ground, it hit an obstruction and broke off short in his hand. He looked at David.

'We could easily jump over it,' he suggested.

'And land on another one, perhaps.' David shook his head, and paused for a moment before adding: 'Now we're in a hell of a mess! That bomb idea was a complete flop—the danger's been scattered all over the place.'

Another cry of pain from the surrounding trees. A rattle of rapid fire began in the distance. A moment later, a section of the door's bottom edge snapped off and began to float away. Hastily, they slammed it shut and slid the bolt.

'We'll have to get out of here pretty soon,' muttered the sergeant.

They gazed speculatively out of the shattered windows. The

sunlight filtered down through the branches to fall on ground which *looked* bare, but ... David turned his attention to the cobwebby space overhead. Safety, for a while at least, seemed to lie up there. With the other's help, he grasped a roof truss and swung himself up. The boarding proved to be in very bad condition, so that he was able, by standing on the beam, to kick a hole through the rotting roof.

Shortly afterwards, the two men sat side by side on the coping, staring through the deserted wood. There was not a man in sight. Far away to the right, they could still hear spasmodic shooting and an occasional cry. David gave a hail, but it brought no answer—there had been too many cries. The firing was slackening now, and he wondered whether the fact indicated escape or defeat.

'I guess we'll have to stay here till somebody turns up,' he said, at length.

The other did not answer; he was staring in fascination at a patch of open ground. Its whole surface appeared to be in motion. Drifting streams of sticks and chips of wood were oozing to several centres. David looked about hastily, and observed the same seeping movement in a number of places.

'There must be dozens of them!'

The sergeant nodded. 'And we're in the middle,' he added. 'And it all comes of this gallivanting about the Universe. I never did think much of it. Stick to your own planet, is what I say; it's quite big enough. But will they? Not so's you'd notice it. They go flinging themselves into space, and then what happens?' He paused aggrievedly. 'They have to go and bring back this blasted thing from Venus! Damn' silly, ain't it?'

In their present predicament, David felt inclined to overlook the future prospects for interplanetary travel which were opened up by the more or less successful return of the *Hurakan*, and agree with the sergeant.

'If we could only see the thing, we might be able to do something,' he grumbled. Then suddenly an idea struck him, and he swung himself back through the hole in the roof. As he searched through the accumulated rubbish, he noticed that a quarter of the door had already gone. An exclamation of satisfaction told the sergeant that he had made a find.

'What is it?'

There was no answer for a while. Finally, David said: 'Can you see the door from there?'

The sergeant found that, by craning over to the limit, this was just possible. David's head and shoulders appeared through the empty window-frame alongside the door. His hand held a battered can of red paint, which he proceeded to pour out, but instead of reaching the ground, it threw the shape which lay there into visibility. It was a mere miniature, but even so, it was a far more alarming object than the aerial photograph had suggested.

CHAPTER FIVE

THE INVISIBLES' SECRET

THE main mass of the creature was hemispherical, with the flat side resting on the ground. The domed top was bare and smooth for more than half-way down its side, but for the rest of the way, it bristled with blunt projections. At the end of each of those was a wide mouth, snapping continuously and full of sharp teeth. David concentrated on one of these 'heads,' and daubed it thoroughly.

He noticed that, if necessary, the wide jaws were capable of opening far back, like those of a serpent. It made him shudder to think of the size of the original invader of the *Hurakan*, though even this little specimen was a long way from being harmless. He was able, now, to see the way in which the mouths wrenched lumps of wood from the door, bolting them whole in the same way that Toby's leg had been bolted. Repulsive as the creature was, it became less perturbingly uncanny than had been the sight of the objects drifting down its unseen throat.

David even felt slightly heartened—one could at least fight a visible enemy. He slopped his paint this way and that, to detect the presence of any other. Only one was within his range, and the section which was revealed showed it to be even smaller than the first; but despite its mere nine-inch diameter, the many mouths snapped no less ferociously. As he leaned yet farther out, a cascade of dirt rattled past his head.

'Hi!' called the sergeant's voice, in some agitation. 'There's one of the darned things up here.'

David scrambled back to the roof, the paint can, which was his only weapon, still in his hand. The sergeant was staring and pointing towards a spot near the centre of the coping. Already, the supports had been laid bare, and a piece of wood was rising into the air. His pot was almost empty, but he flung the last few drops at the place. They were enough to reveal two or three pairs of snapping jaws. The creature was not only on the roof with them, but it was gnawing away at the supports.

He threw the useless can away, and looked around. Branches thrust themselves against the end wall of the hut. It would be a fair jump to the tree-trunk. He looked at the other doubtfully. The policeman grinned as he saw that look.

'Used to do a bit of jumping in the old days, and I'm still good for that distance,' he said.

He led the way to the end, scrambling astride the gable. There was need of hurry, for the whole roof would collapse the moment the creature began seriously on the main tie-beam. He stood there, poised on the extreme gable-end, steadying himself with a hand on David's shoulder. He launched, with a powerful leap, well into the branches.

'Good. Now climb up a bit, and I'll come over.'

He felt his right foot slip as he took off, and heard the sergeant's startled cry. Desperately, he grappled at the branches, only to feel them snap beneath his weight. Something sluggishly yielding broke his fall. Like a flash, he hurled himself to one side and rolled. Even as he went, he heard the tearing sound of fragments of his coat ripping away. The sergeant's voice called after him hoarsely. David sat up, and in that momentary rush of elation which follows a narrow escape, grinned up at him.

'I fell on one of 'em,' he announced. 'What do you know about that?'

'Fell on it?'

'I did; and it's a lucky thing for me that it hasn't got teeth on top. It was right under the tree, and——'

He stopped suddenly, as he noticed that the creature was eating into the tree-trunk. It was not big, he judged, for the floating chunks of wood were no larger than lumps of sugar; nevertheless, the tree was slowly but surely being undercut.

The other had started to descend, but he called to him to stop. With a stick dropped by one of the retreating bombers, he thrashed furiously at the invisible feeder. There was no apparent effect; the wood chips continued to flow neither slower nor faster than before. David calmed himself. At the present rate, it would be some time before the tree fell—that was, if the food did not cause the animal to grow. With a swift inspiration, he thrust a broken branch into the undercut, so that it must be gnawed through before the trunk could be consumed further. Behind him, the roof of the hut collapsed with a startling crash.

'Not much too soon,' he muttered, as he watched the rising cloud of dust.

'Look here,' objected the sergeant, 'I can't stay up here forever.'

'Why not? It's the safest place.'

Another smashing thud caused David to jump around. Less than forty feet away, a tall tree had toppled and fallen. It became uncomfortably clear to both of them that this was not a safe place, after all. The sergeant's perch was overtopped by trees on all sides, many of them already showing deep cuts. Any one of them falling in his direction would certainly sweep him down. He began to descend hastily.

'Wait a minute. You can't come down the trunk,' David told him. Cautiously testing the way before him with his stick, he made for a spot beneath the lowest spreading bough. He thrust all around, and ascertained that the ground was indeed as empty as it looked.

'All clear here; you can drop.' The sergeant obediently landed beside him. 'Now, we've got to get clear of this place at once. The best way will be—good God, what's that?'

There was no need to ask. A crackle of snapping sticks was followed by a swashy thud almost beside them. One of the creatures, caught in the higher branches, had succeeded in eating away its own supports. They backed away in haste. The sergeant pulled out a handkerchief and mopped his damp brow.

'Like a blinkin' nightmare,' he mumbled, looking nervously around and above. 'That was a near thing. I don't like this at all. The inspector said there was only one of the brutes.'

'Did he? Well, he was wrong. So was Captain Forbes. Dirk was the only one of us who had any sense—he cleared off. And that's just what we are going to do now—if we can.'

They began a slow journey. Every foot of the ground had to be tested with sticks, which they waved before them like the feelers of some giant insect. Frequently, they cast anxious glances upwards for fear of another falling creature, or of the trees themselves. An hour and a half of such progress found them more nervy and jumpy than ever. Each had discarded several sticks worn down by constant snapping, and so far, they had encountered no sign of any other survivors. The sergeant paused, and wiped his forehead again.

'We must get clear of 'em soon,' he said, without a great deal of conviction.

'I think there are less of them now,' said David, 'but they're bigger. They've been growing hard all the time we've been getting here. Come on.'

Five minutes later, there came a snap which removed a ten-inch length of David's stick. He recoiled. So large a bite proclaimed it as a monster which should be given a wide berth. They started beating around to one side without any success, and then tried the other. The way ahead proved to be completely blocked by a semi-circle of the snapping invisibles. The only thing left to do was to retrace their steps and detour around the spot.

They turned back, by common consent, and began to trace the path with wavering sticks. The sergeant was in the lead, and he knew that they had an almost straight track for some yards. He was the more surprised, therefore, when he encountered an obstacle straight ahead. He grunted and tried either side, in vain. The two looked at each other.

'We found a way in, so there must be a way out,' David said desperately.

If there was, they both failed to find it. The circle about them seemed complete.

'Listen!' said the sergeant.

For half an hour they had been penned in the diminishing circle, and lusty hails from both had failed to produce any result. Save for the invisible monsters, they might have been alone in the world. Faintly, out of the silence, came an unmistakable 'Hullo!' Both replied with full lung power.

'Coming!' the voice sang back. 'Stay where you are.'

Any other course being impossible, David replied with instructions to hurry; but it took another fifteen minutes before they saw the owner of the voice cautiously approaching. He was a small young man with large glasses, and he whistled cheerfully. One hand waved a long, metal rod before him. Beneath the other arm he clutched a bundle of thin sticks, each tipped with a white knob.

'Hullo! What's wrong with you two?' he asked.

'Surrounded,' answered David curtly. The casual air of the newcomer irritated him considerably.

'Uncomfortable,' commented the young man. 'Never mind. We'll soon have you out of that.'

He thrust with his rod until he encountered the snapping barrier. Snatching a stick from his bundle, he held out the knobbed end. Immediately it had been broken off, he held out other little sticks to left and right to suffer the same fate.

'Who are you?' he asked. The sergeant told him.

'They thought you were done for,' he said, pointing back over his shoulder. 'Most of your lot were.'

Curiosity got the better of David's disapproval of the nonchalant young man.

'What are you doing? Poisoning them?'

'No, we haven't found a suitable poison for them yet. Watch.'

He pointed to the recently swallowed white knob, and they saw that it had turned to a bright blue.

'Methylene blue wrapped in soluble paper,' he explained. 'Away goes the paper and, presto! visibility. My boss, Cadnam, the biologist, had some hundreds of these pills made up. A man called Dirk Robbins came to him in a fearful state, yesterday. Cadnam saw that we'd have to make the brute visible before anything else could be done.'

'Good old Dirk!' enthused David.

The other nodded. 'He had a bit more sense than the rest of you,' he said, ungracefully. 'Unfortunately, by the time we got here, some fool had been feeding fireworks to the brute.'

The blue stain, growing less intense as it dissolved, rapidly spread throughout the creature. They could see, now, not only the domed outline which they had expected, but could look right into it as though it were a stained specimen on a slide. It became easy to trace the many throats to their common stomach, and also to observe a kind of vascular system. At the root of each of the many 'heads,' a kind of valve could be seen rhythmically contracting and expanding. The young man pointed to one of these organs, and shook his head.

'That's what caused most of the trouble,' he explained. But neither David nor the sergeant felt in the mood for a lecture. More than four feet of the creature blocked their way to freedom, and visibility had not interfered in the least with its appetite. They said as much.

'Oh, that's all right,' said the young man cheerfully. He drew a rapier-like instrument from among his bundle of sticks, and set himself to piercing the contractile organs with care and accuracy. As he worked, he continued to explain.

'A very interesting arrangement, not unlike a heart—but the thing only needs one heart really, and it's got scores. It's a kind of composite animal, and when it was blown to bits, every part with a pulse like that became a separate individual. It quickly re-formed, and began to live on its own. When two of them press closely together, they merge again—I expect that that's how you got surrounded. A very primitive form, really. So far as we know at present, the only way of killing them seems to be to put every pulse out of action—as long as there's one left going, it can rebuild itself.'

When he had finished off all the heads he could reach from his side, he tossed the spike over to David. After a few minutes' work, the erstwhile danger became no more than an inert lump of bluish jelly over which they could climb.

'Thank God for that!' said David as they reached the far side in safety. The sergeant grunted, and mopped his brow again. The young man led them back over the way he had come.

'What about the original creature? Was that entirely shattered?' David asked.

'Most of it was, but it's building up again. However, we'll be able to deal with it, now that we can see it. Even I felt it was a bit creepy, at first. Transparency is one thing—invisibility, quite another.'

They came at length to irregular rows of the creatures, already stained. They were still gnawing the trees, but seemed almost harmless when deprived of their armour of invisibility. In the distance was a group of men diligently disposing of the monsters with sharp probes. The young man bade them goodbye.

'Keep straight ahead,' he directed. 'It's clear there. And it would please me if you would tell Captain Forbes what I think of him, when you see him.'

'He's safe?'

'Sure to be. That kind always comes out of it all right.'

He was correct. When they reached a group which seemed to be at the centre of operations, the captain was among it. He seemed to be explaining that the failure of his attack was due to the premature explosion of two of the bombs. Dirk detached himself from the others and greeted them heartily.

'Let's clear out,' he said, a few minutes later. 'The gallant captain now has a theory that it would be quicker to gas the brutes. We'll be safer a few miles away.'

THE MAN FROM EARTH

CHAPTER ONE

CREATURES OF THE VALLEY

ONE of the greatest sights in Takon these days was the exhibition of discoveries made in the Valley of Dur.* In the building erected specially to house them, Takonians and visitors from other cities crowded through the corridors, peering into the barred or glass-fronted cages, observing the contents with awe, interest or amusement, according to their natures.

The crowd was formed, for the most part, of those persons who will flock to any unusual sight, provided it is free or cheap; their eyes dwelt upon the exhibits, their minds were ready to marvel and be superficially impressed, but they had come to be amused and they faintly resented the efforts of the guides to stir them into intelligent interest. One or two, perhaps, studied the cases with real appreciation.

But if the adults were superficial, the same could not truthfully be said of the children. Every day saw teachers bringing their classes for a practical demonstration of the planet's prehistoric condition. Even now, Magon, a biology teacher in one of Takon's leading schools, was having difficulty in restraining his twenty pupils for the arrival of a guide. He had marshalled them beside the entrance, and to keep them from straying, was talking of the Valley of Dur.

'The condition of the Valley was purely fortuitous, and it is unique here upon Venus. Nothing remotely resembling it has been found, and it is the opinion of the experts that nothing like it exists anywhere. This exhibition you are going to see is neither a museum nor a zoo; yet it is both.'

His pupils only half-attended. They were fidgeting to and fro, casting expectant glances down the row of cage-fronts, and craning to see over one another's backs, the more excitable among them occasionally rising on their hind-legs for a better view. The passing Takonian citizens regarded their youthful enthusiasm with a mild amusement. Magon smoothed back the silver fur on his head with one hand, and continued to talk:

'The creatures you will see belong to all ages of our world.

* All Venusian terms are rendered in their closest English equivalents.

Some are so old that they roamed Venus long before our race appeared. Others are later, contemporaries of those ancestors of ours who, in a terrible world, were for ever scuttling to cover as fast as their six legs could carry them. . . .'

'*Six* legs, sir?' asked a surprised voice. Some of the youths in the group sniggered, but Magon explained considerately:

'Yes, Sadul, six legs. Did you not know that our remote ancestors used all six of their limbs to get them along? It took them many thousands of years to turn themselves into quadrupeds, but until they did that, no progress was possible. The fore-limbs could not develop such sensitive hands as ours until they were carried clear of the ground.'

'Our ancestors were animals, sir?'

'Well, er—something very much like that.' Magon lowered his voice in order that the ears of passing citizens might not be offended. 'But once they got their fore-legs off the ground, released from the necessity of carrying their weight, the great change had begun: we were on the upward climb—and we've never stopped climbing.'

He looked round at the circle of eager-eyed, silver-furred faces about him. His eyes dwelt for a moment on the slender tentacles which had developed from stubby toes on the fore-feet. There was something magical in evolution; something glorious in the fact that he and his race were the crown of progress. It was a very wonderful thing to have done; to have changed from a shaggy, six-footed beast to a creature who stood proudly upon four, the whole front part of its body raised to the perpendicular to support a head which looked out unashamed at the world. Admittedly, several of his class appeared to have neglected their coats in a way which was scarcely a credit to the race: the silver fur was muddied and rumpled. But then, boys will be boys; no doubt they would trim better and brush better as they got older.

'The Valley of Dur——' he began again, but at that moment the guide arrived.

'The party from the school, sir?'

'Yes.'

'This way, please. Do they understand about the Valley, sir?' he added.

'Most of them,' Magon admitted. 'But it might be as well——'

'Certainly.' The guide broke into a high-speed recitation which he had evidently made many times before.

'The Valley of Dur may well be called a unique phenomenon.

At some remote date in the planet's history certain internal gases combined in a way yet imperfectly understood, and issued forth through cracks in the crust at this place, and at this place only.

'The mixture had two properties. It not only anaesthetised, but it also preserved indefinitely. The result was to produce a form of suspended animation. Everything which was in the Valley of Dur has remained as it was when the gas first broke out; everything which has entered the Valley since has remained there imperishably. There is no apparent limit to the length of time this preservation may continue.

'Among the ancients the place was regarded with superstitious fear, and though in more recent times many attempts have been made to explore it, none was successful until a year ago, when a mask which would withstand the gas was at last devised. It was then discovered that the animals and plants in the Valley were not petrified, as had hitherto been believed, but could, by means of certain treatment, be revived. Such are the specimens you are about to see: the flora and fauna of a million years ago—yet alive today.'

He paused opposite the first case.

'Here we have a glimpse of the Carboniferous Era. The tree-ferns and giant mosses thriving in a specially prepared atmosphere, continuing the lives which were suspended when Venus was very young. We hope to be able to grow more specimens from the spores of these. And here,' he passed to the next case, 'we see the beginning of one of Nature's most graceful experiments—the earliest form of flower.'

His audience stared in dutiful attention at the large, white blossoms which confronted them. They were not very interested; fauna has a far greater appeal to the adolescent mind than does flora. A mighty roar caused the building to tremble; eyes were switched from the magnolia-like blossoms to glance up the passage in anticipatory excitement. Attention to the guide became even more perfunctory. Only Magon, to the exasperation of his pupils, thought it fit to ask a few questions. At last, however, the preliminary botanical cases were left behind, and they came to the first of the cages.

Behind the bars a reptilian creature, which might have been described as a biped had its tail not played so great a part in supporting it, was hurrying tirelessly, and without purpose, to and fro, glaring at as much of the world as it could from intense, small eyes. Every now and then it would throw back its head and utter a kind of strangled shriek.

It was an unattractive creature with a grey-green hide, very smooth; its contours were almost streamlined, but managed to appear clumsy. In it, as in so many of the earlier forms, one seemed to feel that Nature was getting her hand in for the real job. She had already learned to model after a crude fashion, when she made this running dinosaur, but her sense of proportion was not good and she lacked the deftness necessary to produce the finer bits of modelling which she later achieved. She could not, one felt, even had she wanted, have then produced fur or feathers to clothe the creature's nakedness.

'This,' said the guide, waving a proprietorial hand, 'is what we call *Struthiomimus*, one of the dinosaurs capable of travelling at high speed, which it does for purposes of defence, not attack, being a vegetarian.'

There was a slight pause while his listeners sorted out the involved sentence.

'You mean it runs away?' asked a voice.

'Yes.'

They all looked a little disappointed, a trifle contemptuous of the unfortunate, unhappy *Struthiomimus*. They wanted stronger meat. They longed to see—in safety—those ancient monsters who had been the lords of the planet, whose rumbling bellows had sent *Struthiomimus* and the rest scuttling for cover. The guide continued in his own good time.

'The next is a fine specimen of *Hesperornis*, the toothed bird. This creature, filling a place between the *Archeopteryx* and the modern bird, is particularly interesting——'

But the class did not agree. As they filed slowly on past cage after cage, it was noticeable that their own opinions and that of the guide seldom coincided. The more majestic and terrifying reptiles he dismissed with a curt: 'These are of little interest, being sterile branches of the main stem of evolution— Nature's failures.'

They came at length to a small cage occupied by a solitary, curious creature which stood erect upon two legs, though it appeared to be designed to use four.

'This,' said the guide, 'is one of our most puzzling finds. We have not yet been able to classify it into any known category. There has been such a rush that the specialists have not yet had time to accord it the attention it deserves. Obviously it comes from an advanced date, for it bears some fur, though this is localised in patches, notably on the head and face. It is particularly adept upon two feet, which points to a long line of development. And yet, for all we know of it, the creature might have occurred fully developed, and without any evolution—though, of course, you will realise that such a thing could not possibly happen.

'Among the other odd facts which our preliminary observation has revealed is that although its teeth are indisputably those of a herbivore, yet it has carnivorous tastes. Altogether, a most puzzling creature. We hope to find others before the examination of the Valley is ended.'

The creature raised its head and looked at them from sullen eyes. Its mouth opened, but instead of the expected bellow it produced a stream of clattering gibberish, which it accompanied with curious motions of its fore-limbs. The interest of the class was at last aroused. Here was a real mystery about which the experts could, as yet, claim to know little more than themselves.

The young Sadul, for instance, was far more intrigued by it than he had been by those monsters with the polysyllabic names. He drew closer to the bars, observing it intently. The creature's eyes met his own and held them; more queer jabber issued from its mouth. It advanced to the front of the cage, coming quite near to him. Sadul held his ground; it did not look dangerous. With one foot it smoothed the soil of the floor, and then squatted down to scrabble in the dirt.

'What's it doing now?' asked someone.

'Probably scratching for something to eat,' suggested another.

Sadul continued to watch with interest. When the guide moved the party on, he still remained behind, unnoticed. He was untroubled by the presence of other spectators, since most of them had gravitated to watch the larger reptiles being fed. After a while, the creature rose to its feet again and extended one paw towards the ground. It had scrawled a series of queer lines in the dust. They made neither pattern nor picture; they did not seem to mean anything, yet there was something regular about them.

Sadul looked blankly at them, and then back to the face of the creature. It made quick movement towards the scrawls. Sadul continued to stare blankly. It advanced, smoothed out the ground once more with its foot and began to scrabble again. Sadul wondered whether to move on. He ought, he knew, to have kept with the rest; Magon might be nasty about it. Well, he'd stay just long enough to see what the creature was doing this time. . . .

It stood back, and pointed again. Sadul was amazed. In the dirt was a drawing of a Takonian such as himself. The creature was pointing first to himself and then back to the drawing.

Sadul grew excited. He had made a discovery. What was this creature which could draw? He had never heard of such a thing. His first impulse was to run after the rest and tell them, but he hesitated, and curiosity got the better of him. Rather doubtfully, he opened the bag at his side and drew out his writing-tablet and stylus. The creature excitedly thrust both paws through the bars for them, and sat down scratching experimentally with the wrong end of the stylus. Sadul corrected it, and then leaned close to the bars, watching over its shoulder.

First the creature made a round mark in the middle of the tablet; then it pointed up. Sadul looked at the ceiling, but quite failed to see anything remarkable there. The creature shook its head impatiently. About the mark it drew a circle with a small spot on the circumference; outside that, another circle with a similar spot, and then a third. Still Sadul could see no meaning.

Beside the spot on the second circle, the creature drew a small sketch of a Takonian; beside the spot on the third, a creature like itself. Sadul followed intently. It was trying very hard to convey something, but for the life of him he could not see what it was. Again a paw pointed up at the light-globe; then the fore-limbs were held wide apart. The light ... an enormous light ...

Suddenly Sadul got it. The Sun; the Sun—and the planets! He nearly choked with excitement. Reaching between the bars, he grabbed his tablet, and ran off up the corridor in search of his party. The man in the cage watched him go, and as his shouts diminished in the distance, he smiled his first smile for a very long time.

CHAPTER TWO

THE EARTH-MAN'S STORY

Goin, the lecturer in phonetics, wandered into the study of his friend Dagul, the anthropologist in the University of Takon. Dagul, who was getting on in years, as the grizzling of his silver fur testified, looked up with a frown of irritation at the interruption. But it faded at the sight of Goin, and he welcomed him cordially.

'Sorry,' he apologised. 'I think I'm a bit overworked. This

Dur business gives such masses of material that I can't leave it alone.'

'If you're too busy——?'

'No, no; come along in. Glad to throw it off for a time.'.

They crossed to a low divan where they squatted, folding their four legs beneath them. Dagul offered refreshment.

'Well, did you get this Earth creature's story?' he asked. Goin produced a packet of thin tablets from a satchel.

'Yes, we've got it—in the end. I've had all my assistants and brightest students working on it, but it's not been easy, even so. They seem to have been farther advanced in physical science than we are, and that made parts of it only roughly translatable, but I think you'll be able to follow it. A pretty sort of villain this Gratz makes himself out to be—and not much ashamed of it.'

'You can't be a good villain if you're ashamed,' Dagul observed.

'I suppose not; but it's made me think. Earth seems to have been a rotten planet.'

'Worse than Venus?' asked Dagul bitterly. Goin hesitated.

'Yes, I think so, according to his account—but probably that's only because it was further developed. We're going the same way: graft, vested interests, private traders without morals, politicians without consciences. I thought they only existed here; but they had them on Earth—the whole stinking circus. Maybe they had them on Mars, too, if we only knew.'

'I wonder?' Dagul sat for some moments in contemplation. 'You mean that on Earth there was just an exaggerated form of the mess we're in?'

'Exactly. Makes you wonder if life isn't a disease after all—a kind of corruption which attacks dying planets, growing more and more vicious in the higher forms. And as for intelligence . . .'

'Intelligence,' said Dagul, 'is a complete snare and delusion —I came to that conclusion long ago. Without it, you are wiped out: with it, you wipe out one another, and eventually yourself.'

Goin grinned. Dagul's hobby-horses were much-ridden steeds.

'The instinct of self-protection——' he began.

'—is another delusion, as far as the race is concerned,' Dagul finished for him. 'Individuals may protect themselves, but it is characteristic of an intelligent race that it tries continually, by bigger and better methods, to wipe itself out. Speaking dispassionately, I should say that it's a very good thing, too. Of all the wasteful, destructive, pointless . . .'

Goin let him have his say. Experience told him that it was useless to attempt to stem the flood. At length there came a pause, and he thrust forward his packet of tablets.

'Here's the story. I'm afraid it'll encourage your pessimism. The man, Gratz, is a self-confessed murderer for one thing.'

'Why should he confess?'

'It's all there. Says he wants to warn us against Earth.'

Dagul smiled slightly. 'Then you've not told him?'

'No; not yet.'

Dagul reached for the topmost tablet, and began to read:

I Morgan Gratz, of the planet Earth, am writing this as a warning to the inhabitants of Venus. Have nothing to do with Earth if you can help it; but if you must, be careful. Above all, I warn you to have no dealings with the two greatest companies of Earth. If you do, you will come to hate Earth and her people as I do—you will come to think of her, as I do, as the plague-spot of the Universe.

Sooner or later, emissaries will come. Representatives of either Metallic Industries or International Chemicals will attempt to open negotiations. Do not listen to them. However honeyed their words or smooth the phrases, distrust them, for they will be liars and the servants of liars. If you do trust them, you will live to regret it, and your children will regret it and curse you. Read this, and see how they treated me, Morgan Gratz. . . .

My story is best started from the moment when I was shown into the Directors' Room in the huge building which houses the executive of Metallic Industries. The secretary closed the tall double doors behind me, and announced my name:

'Gratz, sir.'

Nine men seated about a glass-topped table turned their eyes upon me simultaneously, but I kept my gaze on the chairman who topped the long table.

'Good morning, Mr. Drakin,' I said.

' 'Morning, Gratz. You have not met our other directors, I think?'

I looked along the row of faces. Several I recognised from photographs in the illustrated papers; others I was able to identify, for I had heard them described, and knew that they would be present. There is no mystery about the directors of Metallic Industries Incorporated. Among them are several of the world's richest men, and to be mounted upon such pinnacles of wealth means continual exposure to the floodlights of publicity. Not only was I familiar with their appearances, but in common with most, I was fairly conversant with their histories. I made no comment, and the chairman continued:

'I have received your reports, Gratz, and I am pleased to say that they are model documents, clear and concise—a little too clear, I must own, for my peace of mind. In fact, I confess to apprehension, and in my opinion the time has come for decisive measures. However, before I suggest the steps to be taken, I would like you to repeat the gist of your reports for the benefit of my fellow-directors.'

I had come prepared for this request, and was able to reply without hesitation:

'When it first became known to Mr. Drakin that International Chemicals proposed to build a ship for the navigation of space, he approached me and put forward certain propositions. I, as an employee of International Chemicals, and being concerned with the work in question, was to keep him posted and to hand on as much information, technical and otherwise, as I could collect without arousing suspicion. Moreover, I was to find out the purpose for which International Chemicals intended to use the new vessel. I have carried out the first part of my orders to the chairman's satisfaction, but it is only in the last week that I have been able to discover her proposed destination.'

I paused. There was a stir among the listeners. Several leaned forward with increased interest.

'Well,' demanded a thin, predatory-faced man on the chairman's right, 'what is it?'

'The intention of the company,' I said, 'is to send their ship, which they call the *Nuntia*, to Venus.'

They stared at me. Save for Drakin, to whom this was not news, they appeared dumbfounded. The cadaverous-looking man was the first to find his voice:

'Nonsense! Preposterous! Never heard of such a thing. What proof have you of this ridiculous statement?'

I looked at him coldly. 'I have no proof. A spy rarely has. You must take my word for it.'

'Absurd! Fantastic nonsense! You stand there and seriously expect us to believe, on your own, unsupported statement, that I.C. intend to send this machine to Venus? The Moon would be unlikely enough. Either they have been fooling you, or you must be raving mad. Never heard such rubbish. Venus, indeed!'

I regarded the man. I liked neither his face nor his manners.

'Mr. Ball sees fit to challenge my report,' I said. 'This, gentlemen, will scarcely surprise you, for you must know as well as I that Mr. Ball has been completely impervious to any new idea for the last forty years.'

The emaciated Mr. Ball goggled, while several of the others hid smiles. It was rarely that his millions did not extract sycophancy; but I was in a strong position.

'Insolence,' he spluttered at last. 'Damned insolence! Mr. Chairman, I demand that this man——'

'Mr. Ball,' the other interrupted coolly, 'you will please to control yourself. The fact that Gratz is here at all is a sign, not only that I believe him, but that I consider his news seriously to concern us all.'

'Nonsense! If you are going to believe every fairy story that a paid spy——'

'Mr. Ball, I must ask you to leave the conduct of this matter to me. You knew, as we all did, that I.C. were building this ship, and you knew it was intended for space-travel. Why, then, should you disbelieve the report of its destination? I must insist that you control yourself.'

Mr. Ball subsided, muttering indefinite threats, and the chairman turned back to me.

'And the purpose of this expedition?' he prompted. I was only able to suggest that it was to establish claims over territories as sources of supplies. He nodded, and turned to address the rest.

'You see, gentlemen, what this will mean? It is scarcely necessary to remind you that I.C. are our greatest rivals; our only considerable rivals. The overlapping of our interests is inevitable. Metals and chemicals obviously cannot be expected to keep apart. They are interdependent. It cannot be anything but a fight for survival between the two companies. At present we are evenly balanced in the matter of raw materials, and probably shall be for years to come. But—and this is the important point—if their ship makes this trip successfully, what will be the results?

'First, of course, the annexation of the richest territories on the planet, with their raw materials. And later, the importation of these materials to Earth. Mind you, this will not take place at once; but make no mistake, it will come as inevitably as tomorrow. Once the trip has been successfully made, the inventors will not rest until they have found a way of carrying freight between the two worlds at economic rates. It may take them ten years to do it, or it may take them a century, but, sooner or later, do it they will.

'And that, gentlemen, will mean the end of Metallic Industries.'

There was a pause during which no one spoke. Drakin looked round to see the effect of his words.

'Gratz has told me,' he continued, 'that I.C. are convinced their ship is capable of the journey. Is that not so?'

'It is,' I confirmed. 'They have complete faith in her; and so have I.'

Old John Ball's voice rose again.

'If this is not nonsense, why have we let it go on? Why have I.C. been allowed to build this vessel without interference? What is the good of having a man there who does nothing to hinder the work?' He glared at me.

'You mean——?' inquired Drakin.

'I mean that this man has been excellently placed to work sabotage. Why has there been none? It should be simple enough to cause an "accidental" explosion.'

'Very simple,' agreed Drakin. 'So simple that I.C. would jump to it at once—even if there were a genuine accident, they would suspect that we had a hand in it. Then we should have our hands full with an expensive vendetta. Furthermore, I.C. would recommence building with additional precautions, and it is possible that we might not have a man on the inside. I take it that we are all agreed that the *Nuntia* must fail—but it must not be a suspicious failure. The *Nuntia* must sail: it is up to us to see that she does not return.

'Gratz has been offered a position aboard her, but has not, as yet, returned a definite answer. My suggestion is that he should accept the offer, with the object of seeing that the *Nuntia* is lost: the details I can leave to him.'

Drakin went on to eleborate his plan. Directly the *Nuntia* had left, Metallic Industries would begin work on a space-flyer of their own. As soon as possible, she would follow to Venus. Meanwhile, I, having settled the *Nuntia*, would await her arrival. In the unlikely event of the planet being found inhabited, I would get on good terms with the natives and endeavour to influence them against I.C. When the second ship arrived, I was to be taken off and brought back to Earth, while a party of M.I. men remained to survey and annex territories. On my return, I would be sufficiently rewarded to make me rich for life.

'You will be doing a great work for us,' he concluded, 'and we do not forget our servants.' He looked me straight in the eyes as he said it. 'Will you do it?'

I hesitated. 'I would like a day or so to think it over.'

'Of course. That is only natural; but as there is not a great deal of time to spare, will you let me have your answer by this time tomorrow? It will then give us a chance to make other arrangements in case you refuse.'

'Yes, sir. That will do.'

On that, I left them. As to their further deliberations, I can only guess. And my guesses are bitter. . . .

Beyond an idea that it would appear better not to be too eager, I had no reason for putting off my answer. Already I had determined to go—and to wreck the *Nuntia*. I had waited many years to get in a blow at I.C., and now was my chance. Ever since the death of my parents, I had set my mind on injuring them. Not only had they killed my father by their negligence in a matter of unshielded rays, but they had stolen his inventions, and robbed him by prolonged litigation.

Enough, you say, to make a man swear revenge. But that was not all. I had to see my mother die in poverty, when a couple of hundred pounds would have saved her life—and all our money had gone in fighting I.C. After that, I changed my name, got a job with I.C. and worked—hard. Mine was not going to be a paltry revenge: I was going to work up until I was in a responsible position; one from which my hits could really hurt them.

I had allied myself with Metallic Industries because this was their greatest rival, and now I was given a chance to wreck the ship to which they had pinned such faith. I could have done that alone, but it would have meant exile for the rest of my life. Now, M.I. had smoothed the way by offering me a passage home. Yes; I was going to do it. The *Nuntia* should make one trip, and no more.

But I'd like to know just what it was they decided in the Board Room after I had gone. . . .

CHAPTER THREE

THE FATEFUL VOYAGE

THE *Nuntia* was two weeks into space, but nobody was very happy about it.

In those two weeks, the party of nine on board had been reduced to seven and the reduction had not had a good effect upon our morale. As far as I could tell, there was no tangible suspicion afoot; just a feeling that all was not well. Among the hands it was rumoured that Hammer and Drafte had gone crazy before they killed themselves. But why had they gone crazy? That was what worried the rest. Was it something to do with the conditions in space; some subtle, unsuspected emanations? Would we all go crazy?

When you are cut off from your kind, you get strange fancies. Imagination gets overheated, and you become too credulous. That is what used to happen to sailors on their long voyages in the old windjammers, and it began to happen to our crew, out in space. They started to attribute the deaths to uncanny, malign influences in a way which would never have occurred to them on Earth. It gave me some amusement, at the time.

First there had been Dale Hammer, the second navigator. Young, a bit wild at home, perhaps, but brilliant at his job, proud and overjoyed that he had been chosen for this voyage. He had gone off duty in a cheerful frame of mind. A few hours later, he had been found dead in his bunk with a bottle of tablets by his side—one had to take something to ensure sleep, out here. Everyone agreed that it was understandable, though tragic, that he might have taken an overdose by mistake...

It was after Ross Drafte's disappearance that the superstitions had begun to cluster. He was an odd man, with an expression that was frequently taciturn and eyes in which burned feverish enthusiasm. A failure might have driven him to desperation, but in the circumstances he had everything to live for. He was the designer of the *Nuntia*, and she, the dream of his life, was endorsing his every expectation. When we should return to make public the story of our voyage, his would be the name to be glorified through millions of radios, his the face that would stare from millions of newspapers—the conqueror of gravitation.

And he had disappeared.... The air-pressure graph showed a slight dip at one point, and Drafte was no more....

I saw no trace of personal suspicion. No one had even looked askance at me nor, so far as I knew, at anyone else. No one had the least inkling that one man aboard the ship could tell them exactly how those two men had died. There was just the conviction that something queer was afoot.

And now it was time for another....

Ward Govern, the chief engineer, was in the chart-room talking with Captain Tanner. The rest were busy elsewhere. I slipped into Govern's cabin unobserved. His pistol I found in the drawer where he always kept it, and I slipped it into my

pocket. Then I crossed to the other wall and opened the ventilator which communicated with the passage. Finally, after
carefully assuring myself that no one was in sight, I left, closing
the door behind me.

I had not long to wait. In less than a quarter of an hour, I
heard the increasing clatter of a pair of magnetic shoes on the
steel floor, and the engineer passed cheerfully by on his way to
turn in. The general air of misgiving had had less effect upon
him than upon anyone. I heard the door slam behind him. I
allowed him a few moments before I moved, as quietly as my
magnetic soles would allow, to the ventilator.

I could see him quite easily. He had removed his shoes, and
was sitting at a small wall desk, entering up the day's events in
his diary. I thrust the muzzle of the pistol just within the slot
of the ventilator, and with the other hand, began to make
slight scratching noises. It was essential that he should come
close to me: there must be a burn, or at least powder marks.

The persistent scratching began to worry him. He glanced
up in a puzzled fashion and held his head on one side, listening. I went on scratching. He decided to investigate, and released the clips which held his weightless body to the chair.
Without bothering to put on the magnetic shoes, he pushed
himself away from the wall and came floating towards the
ventilator. I let him get quite close before I fired.

There was a clatter of running feet, mingling with cries of
alarm. I dropped the pistol inside my shirt and jumped round
the corner, reaching the cabin door just ahead of a pair who
came from the other direction. We flung it open, and looked
inside. Govern's body, under the impetus of the shot, had
floated back into the middle of the room. It looked uncanny,
lying asprawl in mid-air.

'Quick!' I yelled. 'Fetch the Captain.'

One of them pelted out of the door. I managed to keep my
body between the other and the corpse, while I closed the dead
fingers around the pistol. A few seconds later, everybody had
collected about the doorway, and the Captain had to push
them aside to get in. He examined the body. It was not a
pleasant sight. The blood had not yet ceased to flow from the
wound in the head, but it did not drip as it would on Earth;
instead, it had spurted forth to form several red spheres which
floated freely close beside the corpse.

There was no doubt that the shot had been fired at close
range. The Captain looked at the outflung hand which
gripped the automatic.

'What happened?'

No one seemed to know.

'Who found him?'

'I was here first, sir,' I said. 'Just before the others.'

'Anyone with you when you heard the shot?'

'No, sir. I was just walking along the passage——'

'That's right, sir. We met Gratz running round the corner,' somebody supported.

'You didn't see anyone else about?'

'No, sir.'

'And was it possible, do you think, for anybody to have got out of the room unseen between the time of the shot and your arrival?'

'Quite impossible, sir. He would have been bound to walk straight into me, or the others—even if there had been time for him to get out of the room.'

'Very well. Please help me with this.' He turned to the other four who were still lingering in a group near the door. 'You men get back to work, now.'

Two began to move off; but the other pair, Willis and Traill, both mechanics, held their ground.

'Didn't you hear me? Get along there!'

Still the two hesitated. Then Willis stepped forward, and the Captain's unbelieving ears heard his demand that the *Nuntia* be turned back to Earth.

'You don't know what you're saying, man!'

'I do, sir; and so does Traill. There's something queer about it all. It's not natural for men to kill themselves like this. Perhaps we'll be the next. When we signed on, we knew we'd have dangers we could see, but we didn't reckon with something that makes you go mad and kill yourself. We don't like it—and we're not going on. Turn the ship back!'

'Don't be a pair of fools! You ought to know that we *can't* turn back. What do you think this is—a rowing-boat? What's the matter with you?'

The two faces in front of him were set in lines of stolid determination. Willis spoke again:

'We've had enough, and that's flat. It was bad enough when two had gone, and now it's three. Who's going to be the next? That's what I want to know!'

'It's what we all want to know,' the Captain said meaningly. 'Why are you so anxious to have the ship turned back?'

'Because it's wrong—unlucky. We don't want to go crazy, even if you do. And if you don't turn her back, we damned well will.'

'So that's the way it blows, is it? Who's paying you for this?' the Captain demanded. Willis and Traill remained uncomprehending.

'You heard me,' he roared. 'Who's behind you? Who's out to wreck this trip?'

Willis shook his head. 'Nobody's behind us. We just want to get out of this before we go crazy too,' he repeated.

'Went crazy, eh?' said the Captain, with a sneer. 'Well, maybe they did; and then again, maybe they didn't—and if they didn't, I've got a pretty good idea what happened to them.' He paused. 'So you think you'll scare me into turning back, do you? Well, by God, you won't, you lousy rats! Now get back to your work; I'll deal with you later.'

But neither Willis nor Traill had any intention of getting back. They came on. Traill was swinging a threatening spanner. I snatched the pistol from the corpse's hand, and got him in the forehead. It was a lucky shot. Willis checked, and tried to stop. I got him, too.

The Captain turned, and saw me handling the pistol. The suddenness of the thing had taken him by surprise. I could see that he didn't know whether to thank me or to blame me for so summary an execution of justice. There was no doubt that the pair had mutinied, and that Traill, at least, had meant murder. Strong and Danver, the two men in the doorway, stared speechlessly. Nine men had sailed in the *Nuntia*; four now remained. . . .

For a time, the Captain said nothing. We waited, looking at the two bodies still swaying eerily, anchored to the floor by their magnetic shoes. At last:

'It's going to be hard work for four men,' he said, 'but if each of us pulls his weight, we may win through yet. To the two of you, all the engine-room work will fall. Gratz, do you know anything of three-dimensional navigation?'

'Very little, sir.'

'Well, you'll have to learn—and quickly.'

After the business of disposing the bodies through the air-lock was finished, he led me to the navigation-room. Half to himself, I heard him murmur:

'I wonder which it was? Traill, I should guess. He's the type.'

'Beg your pardon, sir?'

'I was wondering which of those two was the murderer.'

'Murderer, sir?' I said.

'Murderer, Gratz, I said it, and I mean it. Surely you didn't think those deaths were natural?'

'They seemed natural.'

'They were well enough managed, but there was too much coincidence. Somebody was out to wreck this trip and kill us all.'

'I don't see——'

'Think, man; think!' he interrupted. 'Suppose the secret of the *Nuntia* got out, in spite of all our care. There are plenty of people who would want her to fail.'

I flatter myself that I managed my surprise rather well. 'Metallic Industries, you mean?'

'Yes, and others. No one knows what may be the outcome of this voyage. There are a lot of people who find the world very comfortable as it is, and would like to keep it so. Suppose they had planted one of those men aboard.'

I shook my head doubtfully. 'It wouldn't do. It'd be suicide. One man couldn't get this ship back to Earth.'

'Nevertheless, I'm convinced that either Willis or Traill was planted in her to stop us succeeding.'

The idea that both the men were genuinely scared, and wanted only to get back to Earth, never touched him. I saw no reason to let it.

'Anyway,' he added, 'we've settled with the murdering swine now—at the cost of three good, honest men.'

He took some charts from a drawer. 'Now, come along, Gratz. We must get to work on this navigation. Who knows but that all our lives may soon depend on you?'

'Who, indeed, sir?' I agreed.

Another fortnight passed before the *Nuntia* at last dipped her nose into the clouds which had always made the nature of Venus' surface a matter for surmise. By circling the planet several times, Captain Tanner had contrived to reduce our headlong hurtling to a manageable speed. After I had taken a sample of the atmosphere, which proved almost identical with that of Earth, I took my place close beside him, gaining a knowledge of how the ship must be handled in the air.

When the clouds closed in on our windows, to obscure the universe, we were travelling at little more than two hundred miles an hour, and despite our extended wings, required the additional support of vertical rockets. The Captain dropped cautiously upon a long slant. This, he had told me, would be the most nerve-racking part of the entire trip. There was no telling how far the undersides of the clouds were from the planet's surface; he could depend on nothing but luck to keep the ship clear of mountains which might lurk unseen in our path.

He sat tensely at the control-board, peering into the baffling mist, ready at a moment's notice to change his course, although we both knew that the sight of an obstacle would mean that it was too late. The few minutes we spent in the clouds were interminable. My senses drew so taut that it seemed they must snap. And then, when I felt that I could not stand it a moment longer, the vapours thinned, dropped behind, and we swept down at last upon a Venusian landscape.

Only it was not a landscape; for in every direction stretched the sea, a grey, miserable waste. Even our relief could not make the scene anything but dreary. Heavy rain drove across the view in thick rods, slashing at the windows and pitting the troubled water. Lead-grey clouds, heavy with unshed moisture, seemed to press down like great, gorged sponges which would wipe everything clean. Nowhere was there a darkling line to suggest land; the featureless horizon, which we saw dimly through the rain, was a watery circle.

The Captain levelled out and continued straight ahead at a height of a few hundred feet above the surface. There was nothing for it but to go on and hope that we should strike land of some kind. For hours we went on, and for all the difference it made to the scene, we might have been stationary. It was just a matter of luck. Unknowingly, we must have taken a line on which the open sea lay straight before us for thousands of miles. The rain, the vastness of the ocean, and the reaction after our journey through space, combined to drive us into depression. Was Venus, we began to ask ourselves, nothing but a sphere of water and clouds?

At last, I caught a glimpse of a dark speck away to starboard. With visibility so low, I could not be certain what it was, and we had all but passed it before I drew the Captain's attention. Without hesitation, he swerved towards it, and we both anxiously watched it grow.

As we drew closer, it proved to be a hill of no great size, rising from an island of some five or six square miles. It was not such a spot as one would have chosen for a first landing, but he decided to make it. We were all thoroughly tired of our cramped quarters; a few days of rest and exercise in the open air would put new heart into us.

It would be absurd for an Earthman to describe Venus to Venusians, but there are differences between your district of Takon and that island where we landed which I find very puzzling. Moreover, the conditions which I found elsewhere on your planet also differ from those which obtain here. I know nothing about the latitude of these places, but it seems that they must be very far removed from here, to be so unlike. For instance, our island was permanently blanketed beneath thick clouds; one never saw the Sun at all, but for all that, the heat was intense and the rain, which seldom ceased, was warm.

Here in Takon, on the other hand, you have a climate not unlike that of our temperate regions: occasional clouds, occasional rain, warmth that is not too oppressive. When I look round and observe your plants and trees, I find it hard to believe that they can exist on the same planet with the queer jumble of growths we found on the island. I know nothing of botany, so I can only tell you that I was struck by the quantities of ferns and palms, and the almost entire absence of hard-wooded trees.

CHAPTER FOUR

THE SILENT VALLEY

Two days were occupied in minor repairs and necessary adjustments, varied by occasional explorations. These were not pleasure trips, for the rain fell without ceasing, but they served to give us some much needed exercise and to improve our spirits. On the third day, the Captain proposed an expedition to the top of the central hill, and we agreed. We were all to go armed, for though the only animals we had seen were small, timid creatures which scuttled from our approach, there was no telling what we might encounter in the deeper forests which lay between the hill and the beach where the *Nuntia* rested.

We assembled shortly after dawn, almost in a state of nudity. Since the heat rendered heavy waterproofs intolerable, we had decided that the less we wore, the better. It would be hard enough work carrying heavy rifles and rucksacks of supplies in such a climate. The Captain shepherded us out into the steady rain, pushed the outer door to behind us, and we began to tramp up the beach. We had all but crossed the foreshore scrub which bordered the forest proper, when I stopped abruptly.

'Damnation!' I said, with some irritation.

'What is it?' asked the Captain.

'Ammunition,' I told him. 'I put it aside ready to pack, and forgot to put it in.'

'Are you sure?'

I hauled the rucksack off my back and looked through the contents. There was no sign of the packet of cartridges he had given me. In order to travel light, we had only a few rounds each. I could not expect the others to share theirs with me, in the circumstances. There was only one thing to be done.

'I'll go back for them. It'll only take a few seconds,' I said.

The Captain grudgingly agreed. He disliked inefficiency, but could not afford to weaken his party by taking a member of it unarmed into possible dangers. I hurried back to the ship, stumbling along through the sand and shingle. As I pulled open the air-lock door, I glanced back. The three, I could dimly see, had reached the edge of the forest and were standing under such shelter as they could find, watching me.

I jumped inside, and threw down my rifle and rucksack with a clatter. First I rushed for the engines and turned on the fuel taps; then I made forward to the navigation-room. Hurriedly, I set the controls as I had been shown, and pulled over the ignition switch. With my fingers above the first bunch of firing keys, I looked once more out of the windows.

The Captain was pounding across the beach followed at a little distance by the others. How he had guessed that there was anything wrong, I cannot say; perhaps his glasses had enabled him to see that I was in the control-toom. Anyway, he meant business. He passed out of my line of sight, and a moment later I pressed the keys. The *Nuntia* trembled, lurched, and began to slither forward across the sand.

I saw the other two wave despairing arms. It was impossible to tell whether the Captain had managed to scramble aboard or not. I turned the rising ship towards the sea. Again I looked back, just in time to see the others running towards a form which lay huddled on the sand. Close behind it, they stopped and looked up. They shook wild, impotent fists in the direction of my retreating *Nuntia*.

After a few hours, I began to grow seriously worried. There must be other land on this planet, but I had seen none as yet. I began to have a nasty feeling that it would all end by the *Nuntia* dropping into the sea, condemning me to eventual death by starvation should I survive the fall. She was not intended to be run single-handed. In order to economise weight, many operations which could easily have been made automatic had been left to manual control, on the assumption that there would always be one or more men on engine-room duty.

The fuel pressure-gauge was dangerously low, now, but the controls required constant attention, preventing me from getting aft to start the pressure-pumps. I toyed with the idea of fixing the controls while I made a dash to the engine-room and back, but since it was impossible to find a satisfactory method of holding them, the project had to be abandoned. The only thing I could do was to hold on, and hope that land would show up before it was too late.

In the nick of time, it did: a rock-bound, inhospitable-looking coast, but one which, for all its ruggedness, was fringed to the very edges of the harsh cliffs with a close-pressed growth of jungle. There was no shore such as we had used for a landing-ground at the island. The water swirled and frothed about the cliff-foot as the great breakers dashed themselves, with a kind of ponderous futility, against the mighty retaining wall. No landing there.... Above, the jungle stretched back to the horizon, an undulating unbroken plain of tree-tops. Somewhere there I would have to land, but where?

A few miles in from the coast, the *Nuntia* settled it for me. The engines stopped with a splutter. I did not attempt to land her. I jumped for one of the sprung acceleration hammocks, and trusted that it would stand the shock.

I came out of that rather well. When I examined the wrecked *Nuntia*, her wings torn off, her nose crumpled like tinfoil, her smooth body now gaping in many places from the force of the impact, I marvelled that anyone could sustain only a few bruises—acquired when the hammock mountings had weakened to breaking-point—as I did. There was one thing certain in a very problematical future: the *Nuntia*'s flying days were done. I had carried out Metallic Industries' instructions to the full, and the telescopes of I.C. would nightly be searching the skies for a ship which would never return.

Despite my predicament—or perhaps because I had not fully appreciated it as yet—I was full of a savage joy. I had struck the first of my revengeful blows at the men who had caused my family such misery.... The only shadow across my satisfaction was that they could not know that it was I, and not Fate, who was against them.

It would be tedious to tell in detail of my activities during the next weeks. There is nothing surprising about them: my efforts to make the wreck of the *Nuntia* habitable, my defences against the larger animals, my cautious hunting expeditions, my search for edible greenstuffs, were such as any other man would have made. They were makeshift and temporary. I did only enough to assure myself of moderate comfort until the

Metallic Industries ship should arrive to take me off.

So, for six months—by the *Nuntia*'s chronometers—I idled and loafed, and though it may sometimes have crossed my mind that Venus was not altogether a desirable piece of real estate, yet it was in a detached, impersonal way that I regarded my surroundings. It would make a wonderful topic of conversation when I got home. That 'when I got home' coloured all my thoughts; it was the constant barrier which stood between me and the life about me. This planet might surround me, but it could not touch me as long as the barrier remained in place.

At the end of six months, I began to feel that my time of exile was nearly up. The M.I. ship would be finished by now, and ready to follow the *Nuntia*'s lead. I waited almost a month longer, seeing her in my mind's eye, falling through space towards me; then it was time for my signal. I had arranged the main searchlight so that it would point vertically upwards to stab its beam into the low clouds; and now I began to switch it on every night as soon as darkness came, leaving it glaring until near dawn.

For the first few nights I scarcely slept, so certain was I that the ship must be cruising close by in search of me. I used to lie awake watching the dismal sky for the flash of her rockets, and straining my ears for their thunder. But this stage did not last long. I consoled myself, very reasonably, with the thought that it might take much searching to find me; but all day, too, I was alert, with smoke rockets ready to be fired the moment I should hear her. . . .

After four months, my batteries gave out. It is surprising that they lasted so long. As the voltage dropped, so did my hopes. The jungle seemed to creep closer, making ominous bulges in my barrier of detachment. For a number of nights after the filaments had glowed their last, I sat up through the hours of darkness, firing occasional distress rockets in forlorn faith. It was when they were finished that I saw what had occurred.

Why I did not think of it before, I cannot tell. But the truth came to me in a flash: Metallic Industries had duped me, just as International Chemicals had duped my father. M.I. had not built—had never intended to build—a space-ship. Why should they, once I.C. had lost theirs?

That, I grew convinced, was the decision which had been taken in the Board Room after my withdrawal. They had never intended that I should return. . . . I could see, now, that they would have found it not only expensive, but dangerous. There would be not only my reward to be paid, but I might blackmail them. In every way, it would be more convenient that I should do my work, and then disappear. And what better method of disappearance could there be than loss upon another planet? The swine!

Those are the methods of Earth; that is the honour of great companies, as you will know to your cost should you have dealings with them. They'll use you, and then break you. . . .

I must have been nearly crazy for some days after that realisation. My fury with my betrayers, my disgust with my own gullibility, the appalling sense of loneliness and, above all, the eternal drumming of that almost ceaseless rain, combined to drive me into a frenzy, which stopped only on the brink of suicide.

But in the end, the adaptability of my race began to assert itself. I began to hunt, and to live off the land about me. I struggled through two bouts of fever, and successfully sustained a period of semi-starvation when my food was finished and game was scarce. For company I had only a pair of six-legged, silver-furred creatures which I had trained. I had found them one day, deserted, in a kind of large nest, and crying weakly with hunger. Taking them back with me to the *Nuntia*, I fed them, and found them friendly little things. As they grew larger, they began to display remarkable intelligence. Later I christened them Mickey and Minnie—after certain classic film stars at home—and they soon got to know their names.

And now I come to the last and most curious episode, which I confess I do not yet understand. It occurred several years after the *Nuntia*'s landing. A foraging expedition, upon which Mickey and Minnie accompanied me as usual, had taken us into country completely unknown to me. A scarcity of game, and a determination not to return empty-handed, had caused me to push farther than usual.

At last, at the entrance to a valley, Mickey and Minnie stopped. Nothing I could do would induce them to go on. Moreover, they tried to hold me back, clutching at my legs with their forepaws. The valley looked a likely place for game, and I shook them off impatiently. They watched me as I went, making little whining noises of protest, but did not attempt to follow.

For the first quarter of a mile, I saw nothing unusual. Then I had a nasty shock. Some way further on, an enormous head, reared above the trees, was looking directly at me. It was not like anything I had ever seen before, but thoughts of giant reptiles jumped to my mind. Tyrannosaur must have had a head not unlike that. I was puzzled as well as scared. Venus could not be still in the age of giant reptiles, or if she was, I could not have lived here all this time without seeing something of them. . . .

The head did not move; there was no sound. As my first flood of panic abated, it became clear that the monster had not seen me. I took cover, and started to move cautiously closer. The valley seemed utterly silent, for I had grown so used to the sounds of rain that my ears scarcely registered them. At two hundred yards, I came within sight of the great head again, and decided to risk a shot. I aimed at the right eye and fired.

Nothing happened. The echoes thundered from side to side; nothing else moved. It was uncanny, unnerving. I snatched my glasses. Yes! I had scored a bull, right in the creature's eye, but . . . Queer. I decided I didn't like the valley a bit, but I made myself go on. There was a curious odour in the air, not unpleasant, though a little sickly.

Quite close to the monster, I stopped. He had not budged an inch. Suddenly, behind me, I caught a glimpse of another reptile; smaller, more lizard-like, but with teeth and claws which made me sweat. I dropped on one knee and raised the rifle. I had begun to feel an odd swimming sensation inside my head. The world seemed to be tilting about me. My rifle-barrel wavered. . . . I could not see properly. I felt myself begin to fall—I seemed to be falling a long, long way. . . .

When I awoke, it was to see the bars of a cage—

Dagul stopped reading. He knew the rest.

'How long ago, do you think?' he asked. Goin shrugged his shoulders.

'Heaven knows. A very long time; that's all we can be sure of. The continual clouds. . . . And did you see he claims to have tamed two of our primitive ancestors? Millions of years. . . .'

'And he warns us against Earth.' Dagul smiled. 'It will be a shock for the poor devil. The last of his race—though not, to judge by his own account, a very worthy race. When are you going to tell him?'

'He's bound to find out soon, so I thought I'd do it this evening. I've got permission to take him up to the observatory.'

'I'd like to come, too, if you don't mind.'

'Of course not.'

Gratz was stumbling among unfamiliar syllables as the three

climbed the hill to the Observatory of Takon, doing his best to drive home his warnings of the perfidy of Earth and the ways of great companies. He was relieved when both the Takonians assured him that no negotiations between the two worlds were likely to take place.

'Why have we come here?' he asked, when they were in the building, and an assistant, in obedience to Goin's orders, was adjusting the large telescope.

'We want to show you your planet,' said Dagul.

There was some preliminary difficulty due to differences between the Takonian and the human eye, but before long he was studying a huge, shining disc. A moment later, he turned back to the others with a slight smile.

'There's some mistake. This is the Moon.'

'No. It is the Earth,' Goin assured him.

Gratz looked back at the scarred, pitted surface of the planet. For a long time he gazed in silence. It was like the Moon, and yet.... Despite the craters, despite the desolation, there was a familiar quality. A suggestion of the linked Americas stretching from pole to pole.... A bulge which might have been the West African coast.... Gratz gazed in silence for a great while. At last he turned away.

'How long?' he asked.

'Some millions of years.'

'I don't understand. It was only the other day——'

Goin started to explain, but Gratz heard none of it. Like a man dreaming, he walked out of the building. He was seeing again the Earth as she had been; a place of beauty, beautiful in spite of all that man had made her suffer. And now she was dead, a celestial cinder....

Close by the edge of the cliff which held the observatory high above Takon, he paused. He looked out across an alien city in an alien world, towards a white point which glittered in the heavens. The Earth, which had borne him, was dead.... Long and silently he gazed. Then, deliberately, with a step that did not falter, he walked over the cliff-edge....

THE THIRD VIBRATOR

DIANA FRENCH followed a uniformed attendant across a well-kept lawn. Her manner was a blend of eagerness and reluctance, the former but little stronger than the temptation to retreat. The attendant stopped beside a clump of bushes. He pointed ahead.

'Mr. Hixton is over there, madam.'

Diana braced herself and walked with slow deliberation towards a grey-suited figure sagging in a garden chair. She could see that he was lost in reverie, his hands hanging listlessly, his eyes fixed sightlessly on the trees before him.

What twisted thoughts, she wondered, were playing in his brain.

A spasm of panic made her falter. Suppose he were dangerous? Overwork, they had told her, but overwork was not the kind of madness which made people dangerous. She pulled herself together again. There could be no danger, or they would not let her see him alone. She walked on with a firmer step. Three feet behind his chair she stopped and spoke.

'David!'

It was little more than a whisper, but the man stiffened and turned, 'Diana!' he cried.

He rose and took a step towards her, stretching out both hands. She advanced and took them in hers while she searched his face. She had not known what to expect save that he would seem different; but, except for lines of worry, he did not. Her eyes looked deep into his, searching the mind behind them, looking for evidence of what they had told her about him. But there was nothing alien, nothing to show a disordered mind.

Her unconscious stiffness relaxed. She came closer and put her arms about his neck. She tried to speak and failed. The tears she had restrained flooded out.

'They told me,' she said later; 'they told me that—that you——'

'That I was mad?'

She nodded. 'That's what they meant me to think. They said that you had collapsed—had a breakdown through overwork. One of your assistants had found you smashing up your workshop with a sledge-hammer, and they'd had to—send you here.'

'Yes, that's true—but it wasn't madness, my dear. It was a blinding flash of sanity. Another minute, and I'd have finished it.'

'Finished what?'

'Smashing that vibrator. Crushing it into little bits beyond all hope of reconstruction. Alan was too quick, though I don't blame him for stopping me. He didn't know; it must have looked like madness.'

'But, David, why? Why, after all those years of work, should you want to smash it?'

'Because I suddenly knew that if I didn't smash it, it would smash us.'

'Explain, David. I don't understand. I know the vibrator was a weapon, but——'

'Weapon, my dear? Would you call a volcano, an earthquake or a hurricane, a weapon? The vibrator is more than all of these. Its power is unthinkable. It may mean the end of everything, and I—I have let it loose upon the Earth for the third time.'

A worried, doubtful look crept into Diana's eyes. She rested a hand on his sleeve, and gazed closely at him.

'Darling, you must explain; I think you owe it to me. Why did you suddenly want to break up the work of years—an invention which put you at the head of your profession. And what do you mean by "the third time"?'

He looked at her for some moments without speaking. At last he came to a decision.

'I'll tell you. I haven't told anyone else yet—they'd take it as part of my "madness".'

It was a week ago today, he began. Old Fossdyke was making a speech of thanks on behalf of the War Department. It was not an official affair; there were only seven of us round the table, but still it was not entirely informal.

Fossdyke was rolling out phrases, in that admirable way of his, when the feeling suddenly came over me that I had heard it all before. You know that sensation of unplaceable familiarity; everybody knows it. You come suddenly upon a situation, or even a view, which you seem to have seen somewhere, somehow, in the past. The psychologists have an explanation, of course—they always have. But this time the sensation I felt was stronger than ever before.

'This is more than a mere weapon,' Fossdyke was saying. 'It is no adaptation, no improvement of existing methods. It is a breakaway. It is the dream of the scientists come true—it is the death-ray!' He paused.

'And yet,' he added, 'even as the aeroplane when it came was unlike the early dreams of flying machines, so Mr. Hixton's vibrator is unlike what we expected. In our more fanciful moments we pictured, if we gave it any thought at all, something akin to an enormous searchlight sweeping, like a vast scythe, in a destructive arc. Mr. Hixton's invention is, it is true, a directable force, but it is an invisible stream of vibrations which disrupts the ordered vibrations of matter and produces complete disorganisation.

'Without doubt, the potentialities of the discovery are greater than we can now conceive. But I tell you now that Mr. Hixton had achieved what no man in the history of the world has accomplished before. He has ended war. With a weapon such as this, war will be impossible. Its colossal power will make a mockery of all our present arms. From this day, no nation will dare to make use of force. . . .'

I heard Fossdyke's voice booming on, but it seemed to be coming from farther away. My eyelids became unaccountably heavy; not with normal sleepiness, but rather as though a weight were pressing them down. I struggled against the sensation as one does against an anaesthetic—and to as little purpose.

Fossdyke's booming receded farther and farther as my lids dropped lower. By the time they were shut, I seemed to be alone. All external sounds had ceased. I felt that there was nothing about me but a dark, silent void through which I was falling, falling. . . .

How long that sensation continued, I cannot say. There was no means of measuring. I only know that it ended as inexplicably as it had begun. I was aware again of a voice:

'And thus the supremacy of our country was made absolute. While we have this weapon, no race on Earth can face us.'

I opened my eyes in bewilderment. The voice was not Fossdyke's; the language it spoke was not English, yet I understood it. I saw a large hall. I was seated on the foremost of a series of semi-circular benches, all of which were crowded with men and women dressed in gleaming material not unlike silk. Before us, on a throne-like, high-backed chair, sat the speaker.

I was bemused for no more than a few seconds. The memory of Fossdyke began to fade away. I was no longer David Hixton of the twentieth century. I was Kis-Tan, citizen of the mighty Empire of Lemuria. The tall, serious-faced speaker, whom I knew now for Alhui, Chief Councillor of the Empire, continued:

'But it is a two-edged weapon as it exists at present. Therefore I must lay before you a two-fold proposal. First, that all vibrators at present in existence shall be destroyed forthwith. And second, that Kis-Tan shall be granted funds to begin experiments with a view to finding a new type of vibrator, far less drastic in its operation. If, and when, this is accomplished, the new machines shall be retained within Lemuria, where they shall be used only in the event of a dire crisis, and then with the utmost circumspection.'

A murmur of dissent rose from the two hundred or so persons on the benches. Lemuria, already powerful, had been made invincible by the vibrator. To attempt its suppression was, to most minds, like flying in the face of the Sun. The gift of Ra to his chosen people could not thus be spurned.

A number of heads turned in my direction to see how I would take this proposal against my invention. I did my best to make my expression unreadable. Alhui gazed on us calmly, measuring the temper of the council. At length his eyes came to rest on me.

'I shall call first upon Kis-Tan to give evidence,' he said.

I rose and bowed to the golden image of the Sun which blazed on the wall behind him. 'In the sight of Ra, I speak truth,' I said.

'Tell us,' commanded Alhui, 'of the trial of your vibrator.' I turned to face the council, and addressed them.

'When the first vibrator was constructed, I was working to a great extent in the dark. I knew that it was immensely powerful, but I was unable to measure that power. The council, as you will remember, stipulated that the trial of my machine must take place outside the confines of the Lemurian Empire.

'My assistants and I understood and approved of this caution. We travelled a great distance to the south-west until we came upon a sparsely populated country, several thousands of miles from here. The location appeared to be ideal for our purpose. The few men we saw were blacks of a very backward type, and the animals also were primitive, being for the most part marsupials. We decided that any damage we might do would matter but little in such a country. Accordingly we set up the vibrator in an immense plain.

'After we had put on our protective clothing, I myself threw over the switch. The result surpassed even my expectations. There was no visible emanation, no ray, nor was there any sound: nothing to show that there was now in action a vibration which could throw out of phase that other vibration which we call "life." The grass, the leaves, even the trees them-selves, seemed to wither while we watched. Every animal died where it stood; every insect dropped.

'We were all overawed—perhaps a little afraid. Soon, how-ever, our enthusiasm reasserted itself. We conducted a number of tests to prove range, directability, and so on, then moved on to fresh ground for further tests.'

As I paused, Alhui asked: 'You have seen those experi-mental grounds since then?'

'I have.'

'Tell the council of their condition.'

'They were barren. There was nothing but lifeless desert sand.'

I sat down, and there arose a murmur which Alhui quickly quelled. 'I call upon Aphrus, missionary of Ra, in the land of Aegypt.'

A tall, shaven-headed man, wearing a robe much worked with gold thread, arose, saluted the sign of Ra, and began to speak in a powerful, resonant voice.

'In Aegypt, where the people are being weaned from dark superstition and shown the glory of Ra, the Lord of Life, we, priests and converts, worked amid great dangers. When we heard of the vibrator, we petitioned that one should be sent to us for our protection. We were doing all in our power to ensure peace, but we must be prepared for war.

'The inevitable day came when the heathen essayed to con-test the mightiness of Ra. From the south and the west, black men and brown, they marched upon us. We sent messengers to warn them that we were invincible. They killed our mes-sengers. In their hundreds and thousands they advanced—we had no choice but to use the vibrator.

'As the switch was pulled over, they dropped in their legions. In men and horses alike, that vibration which we call life, given of Ra, was quenched. The very trees and flowers drooped and died. The heathen covered the ground with their innumerable bodies. Ra blazed down in great anger on their corpses, and they were corrupted.

'But Ra was displeased also with his servants. From the field a stench arose and floated over all Aegypt, and with it came plague. Out of every four men, three died. When it became safe, we went out to see the battlefield. It had been a pleasant, fruitful land. Now we found it scorched and sandy beneath the pitiless eye of Ra—an arid desert.'

He finished, and walked back to his seat. Calmly, Alhui

called the next witness. 'Yoshin, of the Temple of Knowledge.'

Yoshin stood up. He was a bent, bearded man of great age and spoke in a voice scarcely audible.

'In our mountain fastnesses, we have for centuries pursued pure knowledge. We have been but little molested, for we have not the things which most men value. But more lately we have been disturbed. The brown men to the south-west caused us no anxiety, for they are content to stay behind the mountain barriers, but the yellow race of slant-eyed men to the east and north-east became dangerous.

'Lemuria provided us with vibrators. Many of our members reverted temporarily to a state of less enlightenment. They grew vengeful, and pursued our attackers far to the north-east. As a monument to their folly and their madness, there is now a great desert beyond our northern mountains.'

The next witness was called. He wore a military uniform, and his speech was brief and concise.

'To protect the communications on the west between ourselves and the new colony of Atlantic, I was given a vibrator. In repulsing continual attacks by red-skinned men from the north, several deserts have been created.'

He retired, and Alhui called another witness, and then another. Endlessly it seemed to go on, this tale of deserts large and small created by my machine. And as the recital continued, the temper of the council changed. At last Alhui disposed of the final witness and called upon me again.

'You agree with the council's proposal, Kis-Tan?'

'I do.'

'And you will do all in your power to construct a modified form of the vibrator?'

'It may not be possible, but I will do my best.'

There was a break here in my vision, projected memory, or whatever mental process I was undergoing. Some months—I cannot say how many—had passed, and I was in my laboratory with my assistants.

We had worked hard, and now fancied we had met with success. A fair trial of the new machine we had produced would have been too dangerous, but for a preliminary test, to ensure that the working parts functioned properly, we had constructed a special chamber of stone slabs, lined with insulating material. Into this we moved the machine, with infinite care, and together with it we enclosed growing plants and a few small animals.

I pulled over the switch We intended to give the equivalent

of one minute's exposure to the vibrations. Half the time had passed when the catastrophe came, without warning.

The stone chamber collapsed. Its walls did not merely fall; they seemed to dissolve abruptly into a fine dust. I had a brief glimpse of the machine still standing; then some titanic force gripped and seemed to wrench me apart...

Again that sensation of falling timelessly through a silent, swirling blackness, until suddenly I was aware that I stood upon a solid floor. Before me was a tall window, and I looked down through it on a scene of bustling activity.

Immediately below ran broad, busy streets, and beyond them lay the quaysides of a harbour. Ships were being unloaded there by swarms of hurrying men. Still farther off, ships with sails of red, purple or russet, looking like huge butterflies, were sliding over a blue sea; homeward bound, with a small, joyous white wave curling from the bows. My gaze followed one as it rounded the headland and passed the harbour pylons.

I saw the tumult on deck and the lowering of the vivid scarlet sails, embroidered with the golden emblem of Ra. The wealth of the world was pouring into Zapetl, the greatest port in Atlantis; and I knew that I was Xtan, a person of rank, as was shown by the feathered headdress which I now held in the crook of my left arm. A glittering, embroidered tunic clad me to the knees, while from my shoulders hung a cloak of gorgeous featherwork.

Behind me in the silent room stood two guards, flanking a pair of doors which led to inner apartments. They were rigid as statues of wood and gold; not a movement, not a creaking of their military harness, revealed them for human beings. Even when, with a sudden click, the doors flew wide open, their eyelids did not so much as flicker. Without hesitation, I crossed the room, and as I crossed the threshold the doors slid together once more and refastened themselves.

The room I now entered seemed austere to my Atlantean taste. There was comfort in its chairs and couches, but unnecessary decorations had been discarded. There were none of the prized featherwork pictures essential to any house of social standing, nor were the usual intricate screens visible, while the lighting arrangements, instead of providing an excuse for an orgy of gold-work, were carefully concealed. I approached the far corner, and saluted a figure which sat sunken in a chair.

'You commanded me, Zacta, and I have come,' I said.

Zacta raised his white-haired head and searched my face with a troubled look. He was a very old man; so old that none knew his true age. Even the oldest could remember but little change in him, and in the popular mind he was all but immortal. The wisdom which the phenomenal man had amassed during his longevity had guided Atlantis through many a crisis, until he had come to be regarded as a mixture of oracle and demi-god. There was even a growing superstition that when Zacta should die, Atlantis would fall.

'Yes, Xtan, I sent for you,' he said, still studying my face. He put up a hand and stroked his beard, pausing so long that I became uneasy. At last he said:

'I have been told that you are experimenting with vibrations, with a view to finding a new weapon. Is this true?'

I nodded. 'It is perfectly true—and I have been more successful than I had hoped.'

Zacta shook his head slowly. 'I have always feared this. That vibration should have remained unknown.'

'But you have taught——'

'I have taught you to seek truth, and science is a form of truth. My quarrel is not with your discovery, but with your publication of it. There are some forms of knowledge which it is unwise to spread; men are not yet ready to handle them. They cannot control themselves; how, then, should they be able to control mighty weapons? This knowledge of yours must be suppressed—it is a danger, not a blessing.'

'But——'

Zacta lifted his hand, 'It must be forgotten. I have given the matter my deep consideration, and I know that it may be perilous for Atlantis—for the world.'

I grew angry. My researches had taken considerable time and money. My invention was acclaimed by the military authorities. But if this old dotard were against me, all my work would go for nothing. I knew only too well his power and influence. Scarcely a soul in all Atlantis would dare to disagree with Zacta.

It was plain that the old man was losing his grip. Could he not see that my invention meant the dream of ages come true —the mastery of the world?

He saw my rising temper with increasing displeasure. 'You are not even a pioneer,' he said coldly. 'There was a weapon such as yours in Lemuria.'

'I am not interested in mythology,' I answered contemptuously.

'Lemuria is no myth. It existed as a great empire, greater than Atlantis is today. It discovered a form of vibrator, and though it was wise enough to see the danger, it was not wise enough to suppress the invention entirely. The scientists experimented with a new type. Something went wrong. Matter was disintegrated; the crust of the Earth was weakened so that the volcanic fires burst through. The Earth cracked open; the whole world shook in great paroxysms, and when all was quiet again Lemuria no longer existed.'

'A legend,' I said. 'An exaggerated version of some little local eruption. As for this tale of the great Lemuria—well, it may amuse children as much as any other fantasy.'

Zacta shrugged his shoulders. 'Truth is not altered by belief or disbelief. Lemuria, I say, destroyed herself: it shall never be said that Atlantis destroyed herself.'

We looked deep into one another's eyes, exchanging a challenge.

'You must suppress that knowledge,' he repeated. 'Vibrators most not be built.'

I laughed. 'Your information is out of date. Six vibrators have already been built and mounted.'

The old man sagged farther in his chair. He looked even older; his eyes were tragic as he stared. At last he asked: 'Where are they mounted?'

'They are strung along the east coast from Azco,' I told him. 'It is a chain of defence against attack from beyond the Pillars of Hercules. The barbarians in Aegypt and the countries round its sea have become restive. They are jealous of our prosperity, and sooner or later they will attack us. The vibrators will strike their crews and their rowers dead, and not a drop of Atlantean blood will be spilt. Think of that, Zacta; thing of that mastery, and then you will see what the vibrators really mean to us.'

Zacta answered slowly: 'Truly, you have limited vision. How long will your machines remain mere defensive weapons? How long will it be before they are carried out into the world to conquer; to spread death, destruction and deserts? No, I say; the vibrators shall be destroyed.'

'And I say they shall not.'

We faced each other tensely. Zacta's eyes grew hard and menacing. A youthful strength and purpose seemed to shine in them. I knew that he saw Atlantis, perhaps all culture, hanging upon our decision. So did I, but from the opposite angle.

His blue-veined, fragile hand began to move towards his side. I was younger and quicker on the draw. There was a faint 'phut' from my hand-tube. Zacta's tube clattered on the floor. He fell forward with a little feathered dart in his heart. . . .

I stood for a moment scarcely conscious of what I had done. Then as I gazed at his slumped form, the true enormity of the thing came home to me. I had killed the greatest man in all Atlantis. Yet I was but the instrument of his destruction; the true contest had been between Zacta and my vibrator—and the vibrator had claimed the wisest of men as its first victim. Somehow I began to think of my machine as a sentient creature; I was fighting to protect the thing to which my brain had given birth.

I glanced swiftly round the room. There had not been noise enough to alarm the guards, but they were posted outside the only door. Could I march out, trusting to bluff? The risk would be great, for I did not know Zacta's usual method of dismissing his visitors.

The window offered more hope, providing that I was not noticed from the street. I decided that it was safer than an attempt to pass the guards. Impatiently, I kicked off my sandals and fastened them to my belt; then, thankful that Zacta's austere taste had not caused him to remove the decoration from his house-front, I grasped the scrolled stonework beside the window and began to climb.

Luckily, there was only one floor between me and the roof, for though the carving offered easy holds, I was in bad form for such exercise; moreover, I was afraid of becoming giddy. It was with intense thankfulness that I at last pulled myself across the coping. There was little time to waste. I had no idea when someone would enter Zacta's room and find the body.

As swiftly as I could, I refixed my sandals and looked for the roof door. It was not difficult to find, and luck was with me, for it was unlocked. At the top of the stairs I pulled myself together, and began to descend with an appearance of unhurried dignity.

In the forecourt my car waited, balancing on its gyroscopes. I approached it unmolested and slid thankfully into the driving-seat. The hand which I put out for the steering-stick was trembling violently. The gates opened before me, and I jerked the machine forward.

So far, so good. But where was I to go? When Zacta's body should be found, every man and woman in Atlantis would be against me. Every man . . . ? No, perhaps some of my assistants would understand. The vibrator meant everything to them. They would realise that obedience would have caused all our work of years to go for nothing.

Tlantec, my head assistant, was near Azco, where he had been superintending the erection of the vibrators. A glance at the indicators showed me that the batteries were almost full; there would be more than enough power to take me to Azco. I made to the east side of Zapetl and opened flat out. The little gyro-car gave everything she had.

Some hours later, I slid to a stop outside the control-house on the cliffs above Azco. Over the house towered Number One Pylon, supporting the greatest of the vibrators. Far to the north I could see a similar, though smaller pylon, the second of the chain we had erected.

Before I could climb out of the car, the door of the house opened. Tlantec, with a dart-tube in his hand, stood facing me. I knew that the news had reached him.

'Zacta is dead,' he said. 'They say you killed him.'

I began to explain, and Tlantec's eyes grew wide as he listened. When I spoke of Zacta's ban on the vibrators, he stared incredulously.

'But why—why?'

I repeated the old man's words, and he frowned.

'He must have been mad. The greatest power in all the ages to be thrown away for an old wives' tale!'

'And so,' I finished, 'it came to that. Nothing would alter Zacta's mind once it was made up. Either he or the vibrator had to be destroyed.'

There was a considerable pause. I waited anxiously for Tlantec's decision, for my immediate fate was in his hands. If he should choose to shoot me where I stood, he would be acclaimed a national hero. He lowered the tube slowly, gazed at it in a half absence of mind, and then turned his eyes back to me.

'You were right, Xtan,' he said, 'but I wish there had been some other way.'

I nodded. 'So do I—but you know Zacta's power. There was no other way.'

We walked together into the house. 'And now?' he asked.

'We must communicate at once with the other pylons. If necessary, the vibrators must fight against their own destruction. As soon as it is known that I am here we shall be attacked.'

Tlantec looked white. 'You mean that we must turn the machines to landward—train them on our own people?'

'How else can we protect them?'

He went away to call up the other pylons, while I searched for some badly-needed food. He was gone perhaps half an hour. When he came back, it was with a serious expression.

'Pylons 2, 3 and 5 are agreed to stand with us,' he reported, 'but numbers 4 and 6 are opposed. They say that if Zacta condemned vibrators, then vibrators must be destroyed, and they will obey him.'

I thought rapidly. If pylons 4 and 6 were to turn their machines on us, it would be the end. 'Quick,' I said, 'get the protection suits.'

While I was still struggling into mine, Tlantec had fastened his and gone to the window. He called me to him and pointed down to the town. Even at this distance of three miles it was plain that something unusual was taking place.

From the city gates a crowd of men and women was hurrying along the road towards us. Either Pylon 4 or Pylon 6 must have informed the town where I was to be found, and the crowd was out to avenge Zacta. I hurried to the message machine and made connection with the military barracks in Azco.

'Xtan speaking,' I called. 'Head back your people, or I will not be responsible for the consequences.'

I crossed to the big control wheel in the middle of the room and spun it. The big vibrator far above swung slowly to face the town. Tlantec was looking very pale.

'But this is only a mob—unarmed,' he protested.

'A mob is capable of destroying the vibrator. They must be stopped. Switch on minimum power.'

He obeyed with reluctance. The crowd was as yet out of range, and we watched intently. A mile and a half away from us they came to a stop. Those in front were behaving queerly, staggering and moving with queer, twitching, wooden actions. The vibrations at that distance were too weak to kill them, but strong enough to disorganise their movements. Those behind did not understand what was happening, and relentlessly pushed forward; several of the leaders dropped and lay still.

Those to the rear suddenly realised what they faced. They surged to and fro in panic, then broke and retreated pell-mell. The message machine rang stridently.

'Pylon Number 2 speaking. Have you gone mad, Xtan?'

'The vibrators must be saved—at any cost.'

The reply was bitter. 'You have killed a score of unarmed men already, Xtan. We won't stand for massacring our own countrymen.'

'But if they get close they'll wreck us,' I said desperately.

The voice answered with a sneer. 'Are you sure it's not your own skin you're worrying about? You murdered Zacta. Pylon Number 2 is quitting, and the rest will, too.'

The machine went dead. Tlantec spoke from the window. 'They're running back into the town.'

Following his words came a whine overhead, followed by a dull, distant boom. We looked at each other. The guns behind Azco had opened up. There was only one way for us to silence them. 'Full power on the vibrator.' I ordered.

Tlantec did not move. He stared at me with a curious intentness. 'We should destroy all Azco,' he protested again.

'Those guns must be stopped,' I insisted.

'Every man in the town and for miles around would die. You must be mad. Think of the consequences, man! You'd ruin the country.'

I shrugged my shoulders and walked across to the switchboard. What were a few lives? To me, at that moment, no price seemed too big to pay for the preservation of the vibrator. But before I could pull over the handle Tlantec was upon me.

The force of his attack hurled me to the floor, but he could get no hold on the cumbersome garments I wore. I wrenched free and rolled to one side, but before I could rise he was on me again, hammering with futile fists against the heavy clothing. I groped desperately for my dart-tube, only to remember that it was inside my suit, out of reach. With a heave and a twist, I managed to roll uppermost again.

Both of us were breathing hard, for the suits were weighty. I sought with clumsy gloves for his throat, but when I found it, it was impossible to get a grip. Swiftly I changed my tactics and began to fumble for the fastenings of his suit. The vibrator was still at minimum power and directed towards the town, but here, right below it, there might be sufficient radiation to do the job....

Tlantec felt my change of plan and knew what I was after. His struggles grew still more desperate, swinging me from side to side in an effort to throw me off, and causing my groping hands to slip again and again from the fastener. At last I managed to get a finger through the ring, and at that moment Tlantec put forth his mightiest effort. The heave he gave sent me flying to one side, but my finger remained crooked in the ring, and as I went his suit was ripped open. I felt him quiver as the vibrator did its work. He never moved again.

I struggled up, dizzy and panting. Another rumbling boom reached me. How many shots had been fired while we struggled, I could not tell. It was surprising that the pylon had not been hit already. With an effort, I lurched across the room and pulled the full-power switch. I let it stay for a minute before I pushed it back into place and crossed to the windows.

The sight I encountered shocked even me. For as far as I could see, the country was devastated. The vibration had withered grass, leaves, bushes and flowers alike. They drooped and sagged, where a few minutes ago they had proudly waved.

I turned my gaze towards Azco. The city was lifeless; men lay where they had fallen in the streets. The only moving thing was the smoke which still rose from untended fires. On the road in the foreground was a tangle of men and women; a minute ago they had been a crowd in full flight, but none of them would ever run again. In the harbour, vessels still with the wind in their sails sped unguided, to ram one another or to crash upon the stone quays. But—and most important to me—the guns had been silenced. The vibrator was safe.

I crossed back to the board and switched it off entirely. There was no longer need even of minumum power. Within miles of me was nothing living.

I went outside and looked up at the great vibrator. My right hand came up in a salute.

My memory of time is hazy, but I know that it was two or three days later that I saw something moving in the distance. I fetched field-glasses, and managed to make out a marching column of men advancing from the interior. They wore uniforms, but of no regiment which I knew; moreover, they were accompanied by unfamiliar machines.

Evidently the attack was beginning. I had expected it. I would let them get a little closer, and then blast them out of existence. I waited impatiently, filled, not with the desire to kill, but with the determination to assert the supremacy of my vibrator—the greatest power in the world, the triumph of man's genius. 'At ten miles,' I said aloud, 'you shall conquer them.'

But the marchers were still twelve miles away when my patience gave out. They seemed to be in no hurry to attack. Once more I laid my hand on the power switch. 'Now show them who is master,' I cried, as I pulled it over.

I took but one glance before the field-glasses dropped to the floor. The advance had not stopped. The men were plodding on as deliberately as before. A hurried glance at the dials assured me that the machine was working perfectly. What, then, could have happened?'

Suddenly, I had it. Those unfamiliar uniforms were insulating suits. One of the other pylon commanders had given away the secret. The vibrator was straight upon them. How long, I wondered, would the suits withstand its full force? I myself was only assailed by reflected vibrations, and safe enough. All I could do was to keep the machine at full on and trust to time.

Half an hour later they were still advancing. I began to lose hope. For all appearances, the vibrator might as well have been inactive. I smiled rather bitterly when I recalled that the longest time we had dared run even a small vibrator in our tests had been two minutes. We had not known what we had feared, but we had feared something. Then, suddenly, that something began to happen.

Five miles away, the ground split from a centre in radiating crevasses. A large circle crumbled away to dust before my eyes, leaving a vast, shallow bowl. But the bowl did not remain shallow; its bottom continued to crumble and to sink. I saw the men far beyond it halt in dismay and turn back, hurrying as best they could in their heavy clothing.

A violent shaking of the ground sent me to the floor. The pylon above rocked and groaned, but it did not fall. I crawled across the room and threw out the vibrator's switch, but as I did it, I knew it was too late. Zacta had been right. My vibrator was bigger than I knew; it could not only take life, but by prolonged exposure it could disintegrate matter.

The shallow bowl had now become a stupendous shaft. The internal pressures were shifting. Another shock set the whole room shivering. I staggered back to the window. The ground had heaved and was cracked in all directions. What had I done? What had I started? A cataclysm which would shake the world: which might destroy all Atlantis!

A still greater shock made me clutch the window frame. The mighty cliffs to the north had split asunder; up the cleft the sea was roaring in one stupendous wave. From inland came a spurt of livid flame, searing the heavens. The internal fires were loosed. . . .

David Hixton paused, and then he added:

'The next thing I heard was old Fossdyke's voice. It was still booming away about "this weapon which will give us the mastery of the world." I could not stand it. I got up and ran from the room. I did not stop running until I had reached my workroom, for there was only one thought in my mind. I must smash the vibrator. . . .

'Kis-Tan had let it loose on Lemuria. Where is Lemuria? Xtan had let it loose on Atlantis. Where is Atlantis? No one should say that Hixton had loosed it again.

'I went at it with a sledge-hammer, but Alan heard me and came in too soon. And now they've got it. In ten years, or less, every man will be reviling my name—every man, that is, who is still left alive.'

Diana put a hand over his.

'My dear, they have not got it all. Only part of it. You smashed some important piece—I don't know what piece, nor do they. They can't make it work.'

David looked up at her, half-comprehending. 'They can't——?'

'No, dear, it's useless. None of your assistants knows enough to help them.'

David's eyes brightened, his face twisted. He began to laugh, and the tears trickled down his cheeks. Diana stared while the laughter grew wilder and louder. Aghast, she tried to silence him, but the laughter and the sobbing both increased. Two attendants came hurrying across the lawn. One of them attempted to soothe David from his paroxysm. The other took her away.

'You've let him excite himself too much,' he said, accusingly.

'But he isn't mad,' said Diana. 'Not really mad.'

The attendant listened for a moment to the hysterical laughter behind him. He shook his head.

'Well, that all depends on what you call madness,' he said.

WANDERERS OF TIME

John Wyndham wrote strong, imaginative fiction years before fame came his way, and this is a collection of some of his pieces from those days.

Already remarkable are his sense of movement, his sense of invention, his sense of style. The title story of this collection foreshadows frighteningly such later novels as THE KRAKEN WAKES and THE MIDWICH CUCKOOS with its suggestion of time when man is no longer the dominant creature on Earth.

And *The Last Lunarians* and *Derelict of Space* show how well he researched his material, long before space ships had struck out for the moon and the idea of inter-planetary travel had become commonplace.

This is truly another fascinating piece of evidence of John Wyndham's remarkable talent as seer and story-teller.

He was an anachronism
—a Twentieth Century man in a world of androids

Edmund Cooper

THE UNCERTAIN MIDNIGHT

They called him the Survivor—a 20th Century man
'reborn' in 2113. After a devastating atomic holocaust,
mankind had now turned to the machine to solve his
problems. Which led to the androids—descended from
the robot, they were hardly distinguishable from real
humans. By the year 2113 they ran society—leaving
man to a life of leisure.

It was into this world that John Markham emerged
after spending 146 years of suspended animation in
an underground deep-freeze unit. But his new lease
on life was likely to be a short one. A man with his
'outdated' ideas could be very dangerous—a fact the
androids realized only to well . . .

'He writes with great authority and skill'

Arthur C. Clarke

Alfred Coppel

DARK DECEMBER

Begins where *Dr Strangelove* and *Fail Safe* left off . . .
Major Ken Gavin had only one thought when peace
was declared—had his wife and daughter in California
survived the onslaught of Russian ICBMs?

Making his way slowly towards them with whatever
transport he can commandeer, Gavin witnesses the full
horror of the holocaust—grotesque craters where towns
used to be, the ever-present odour of death and disease
and, most sinister of all, the recourse of the surviving
populace to tribal, vigilante ways. Driven forward by a
powerful, innate homing instinct, Gavin survives all this
and goes on to a reunion which is at once tragic and
triumphant.

This account of one man's reaction when the unthinkable
happens with unspeakable results is an unforgettable
reading experience.

Edmund Cooper

TRANSIT

A man without purpose on a voyage of discovery.
He was the subject of an experiment seventy light years
away from Earth. It lay in the grass, tiny and white and
burning. He stooped, put out his fingers. And then, in an
instant, there was nothing. Nothing but darkness and
oblivion. A split second demolition of the world of
Richard Avery.

From a damp February afternoon in Kensington
Gardens, Avery is precipitated into a world of apparent
unreason. A world in which his intelligence is tested by
computer, and in which he is finally left on a strange
tropical island with three companions, and a strong
human desire to survive.

But then the mystery deepens; for there are two
moons in the sky, and the rabbits have six legs, and
there is a physically satisfying reason for the entire
situation.

'He writes with great authority and skill'

Arthur C. Clarke

THE BEST IN SCIENCE FICTION
FROM CORONET

Alfred Coppel
☐ 14809 8   DARK DECEMBER   25p

Algis Budrys
☐ 04399 7   THE IRON THORN   20p

Ed. Groff Conklin
☐ 02880 7   SEVEN COME INFINITY   17½p
☐ 02482 8   13 GREAT STORIES OF SCIENCE FICTION   30p
☐ 10866 5   7 TRIPS THROUGH TIME AND SPACE   30p

Edmund Cooper
☐ 02860 2   ALL FOOL'S DAY   17½p
☐ 15132 3   THE UNCERTAIN MIDNIGHT   25p
☐ 12975 1   SEA-HORSE IN THE SKY   25p
☐ 16217 1   KRONK   30p
☐ 16464 6   TRANSIT   30p

Christopher Hodder-Williams
☐ 16666 5   FISTFUL OF DIGITS   35p

Leo P. Kelley
☐ 16713 0   MINDMIX   30p

Kurt Vonnegut Jnr
☐ 02876 9   THE SIRENS OF TITAN   30p

John Wyndham
☐ 15834 4   THE SECRET PEOPLE   30p
☐ 15835 2   STOWAWAY TO MARS   30p
☐ 17306 8   WANDERERS OF TIME   30p

All these books are available at your bookshop or newsagent, or can be ordered direct from the publisher. Just tick the titles you want and fill in the form below.

CORONET BOOKS, Cash Sales Department, P.O. Box 11 Penryn, Cornwall.

Please send cheque or postal order. No currency, and allow 7p per book (6p per book on orders of five copies and over) to cover the cost of postage and packing in U.K., 7p per copy overseas.

Name...

Address..

....